POWER CODERS

THE SIMULATED FRIEND

AMANDA VINK

ILLUSTRATED BY JOEL GENNARI

PowerKiDS
press™

New York

Published in 2019 by The Rosen Publishing Group, Inc.
29 East 21st Street, New York, NY 10010

First Edition

Illustrator: Joel Gennari
Interior Layout: Tanya Dellaccio
Managing Editor: Nathalie Beullens-Maoui
Editorial Director: Greg Roza

Library of Congress Cataloging-in-Publication Data

Names: Vink, Amanda, author.
Title: The simulated friend / Amanda Vink.
Description: New York : PowerKids Press, 2019. | Series: Power Coders | Includes index.
Identifiers: LCCN 2017057851| ISBN 9781538340172 (library bound) | ISBN
    9781538340189 (pbk.) | ISBN 9781538340196 (6 pack)
Subjects: | CYAC: Computer programming–Fiction. | Morse code–Fiction. |
    Friendship–Fiction.
Classification: LCC PZ7.1.V58 Sim 2019 | DDC [Fic]–dc23
LC record available at https://lccn.loc.gov/2017057851

Manufactured in the United States of America

CPSIA Compliance Information: Batch CS18PK: For Further Information contact Rosen Publishing, New York, New York at 1-800-237-9932

CONTENTS

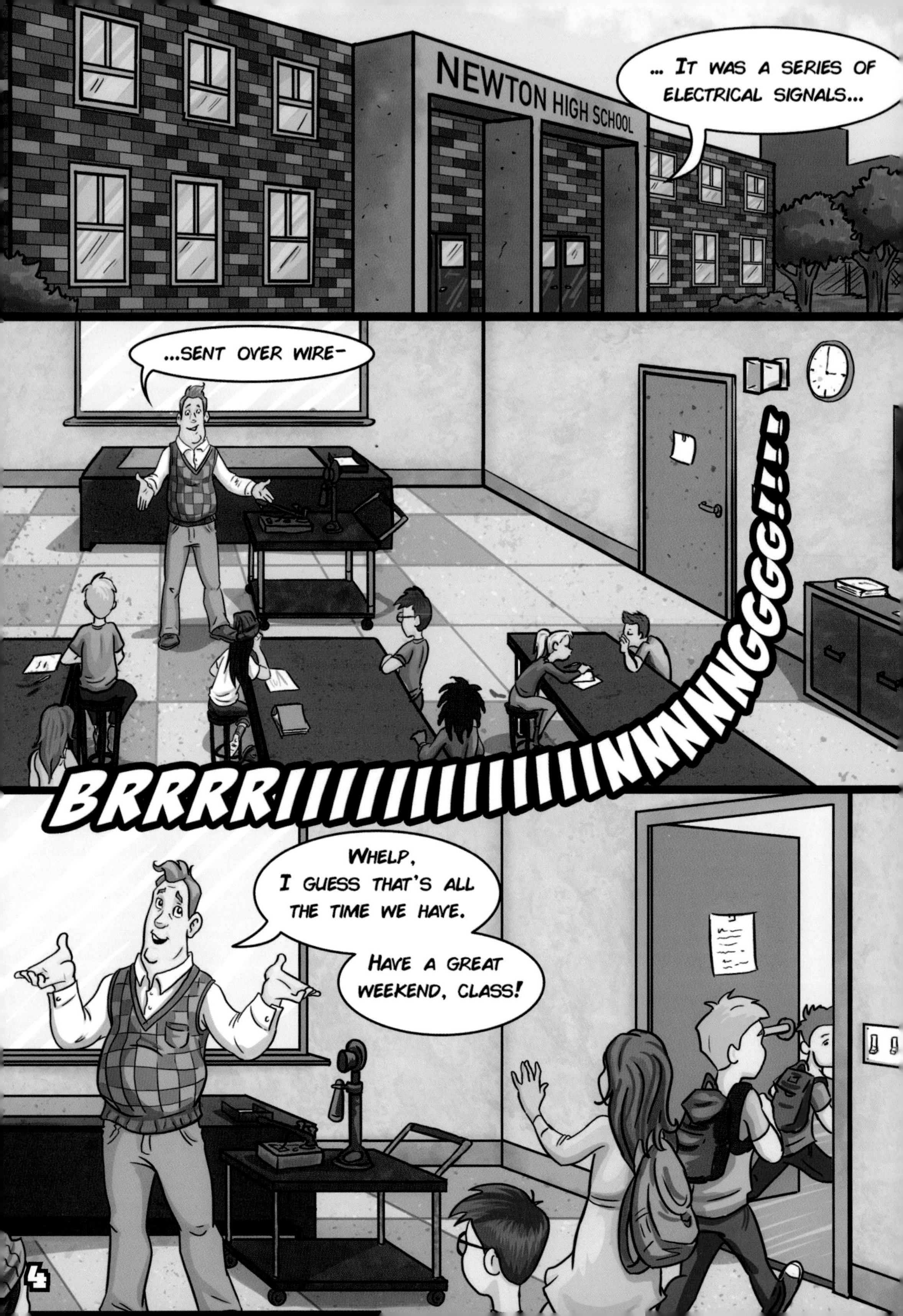
NEWTON HIGH SCHOOL
... IT WAS A SERIES OF ELECTRICAL SIGNALS...
...SENT OVER WIRE-
BRRRRIIIIIIIIIIIIIIIIINNNNNGGG!!!!
WHELP, I GUESS THAT'S ALL THE TIME WE HAVE.
HAVE A GREAT WEEKEND, CLASS!

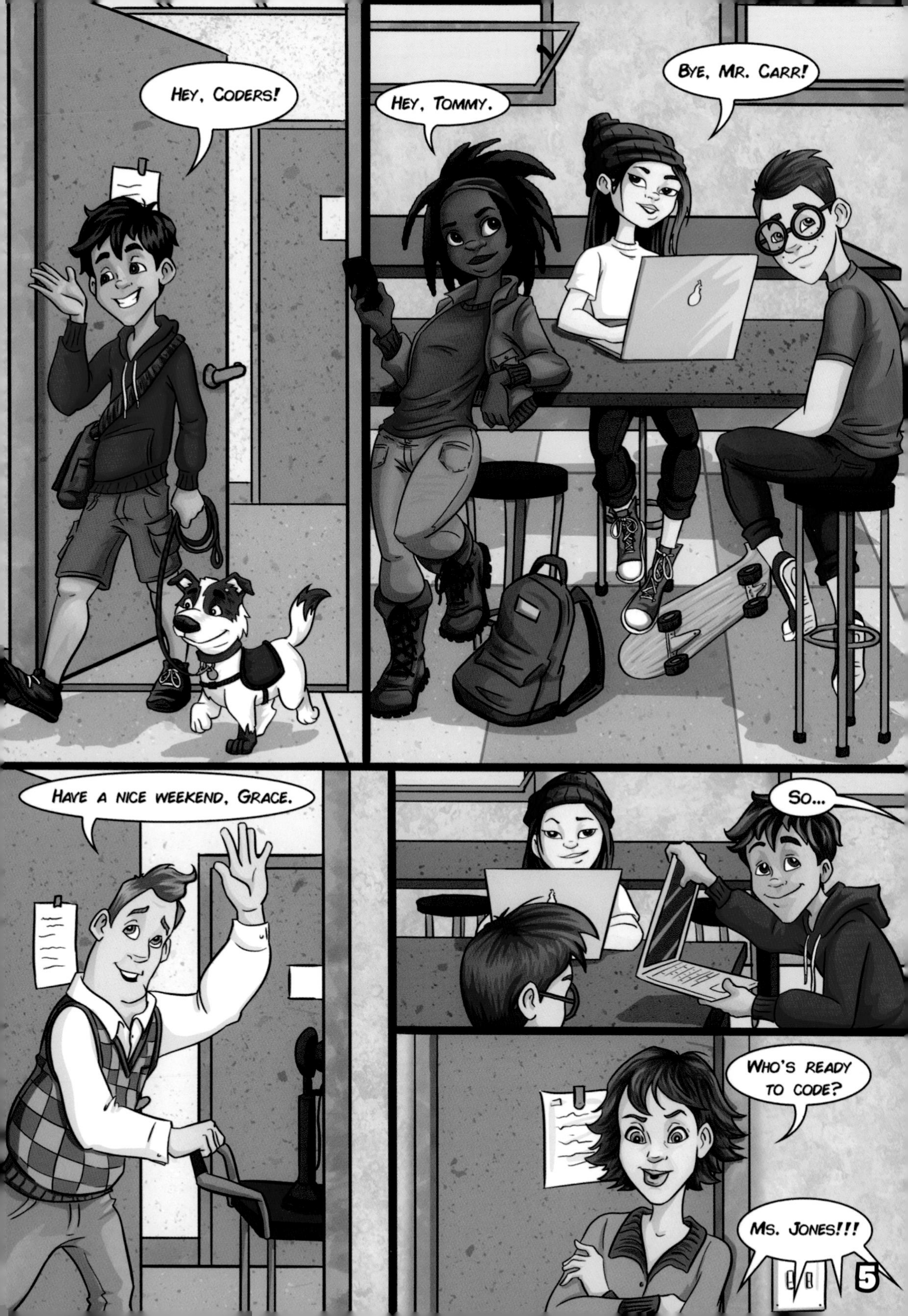
HEY, CODERS!
HEY, TOMMY.
BYE, MR. CARR!
HAVE A NICE WEEKEND, GRACE.
SO...
WHO'S READY TO CODE?
MS. JONES!!!

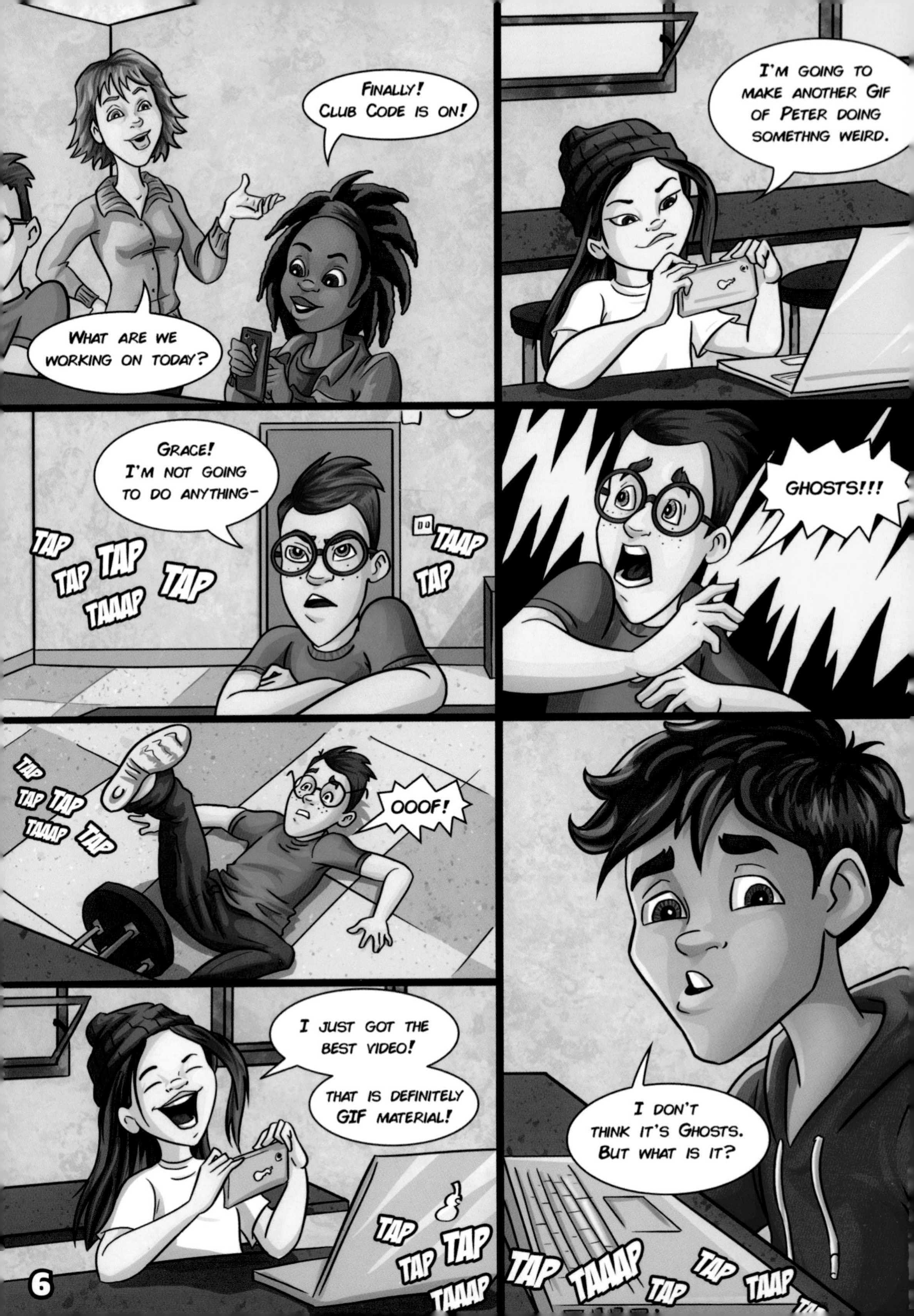

Finally! Club Code is on!
What are we working on today?
I'm going to make another Gif of Peter doing somethng weird.
Grace! I'm not going to do anything-
TAP TAP TAP TAAAP TAP
TAAP TAP
GHOSTS!!!
TAP TAP TAP TAAAP TAP
OOOF!
I just got the best video!
that is definitely GIF material!
TAP TAP TAP TAAAP
I don't think it's Ghosts. But what is it?
TAP TAAAP TAP TAP TAAP

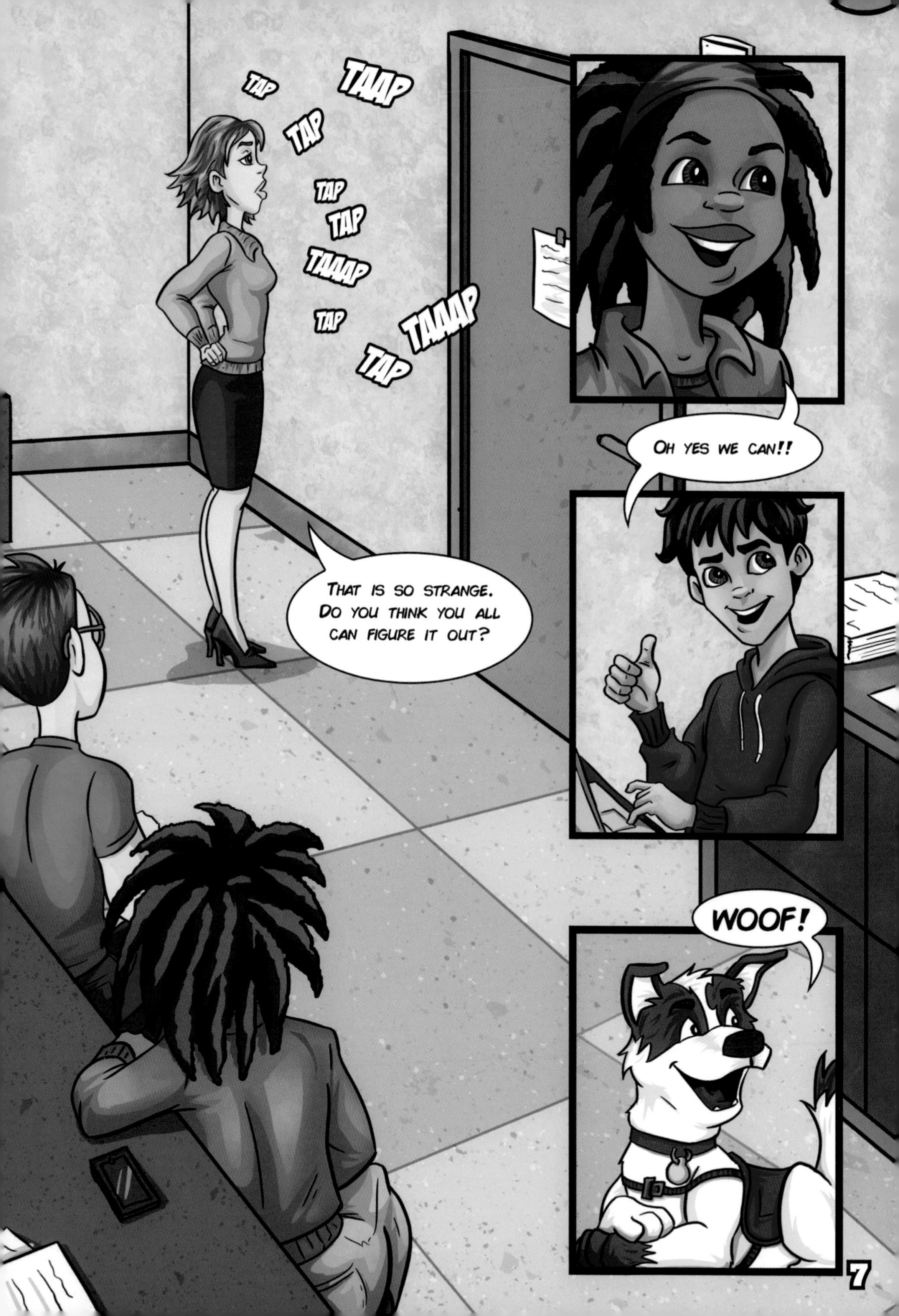
TAP
TAAP
TAP
TAP
TAP
TAAAP
TAP
TAAAP
TAP
THAT IS SO STRANGE. DO YOU THINK YOU ALL CAN FIGURE IT OUT?
OH YES WE CAN!!
WOOF!

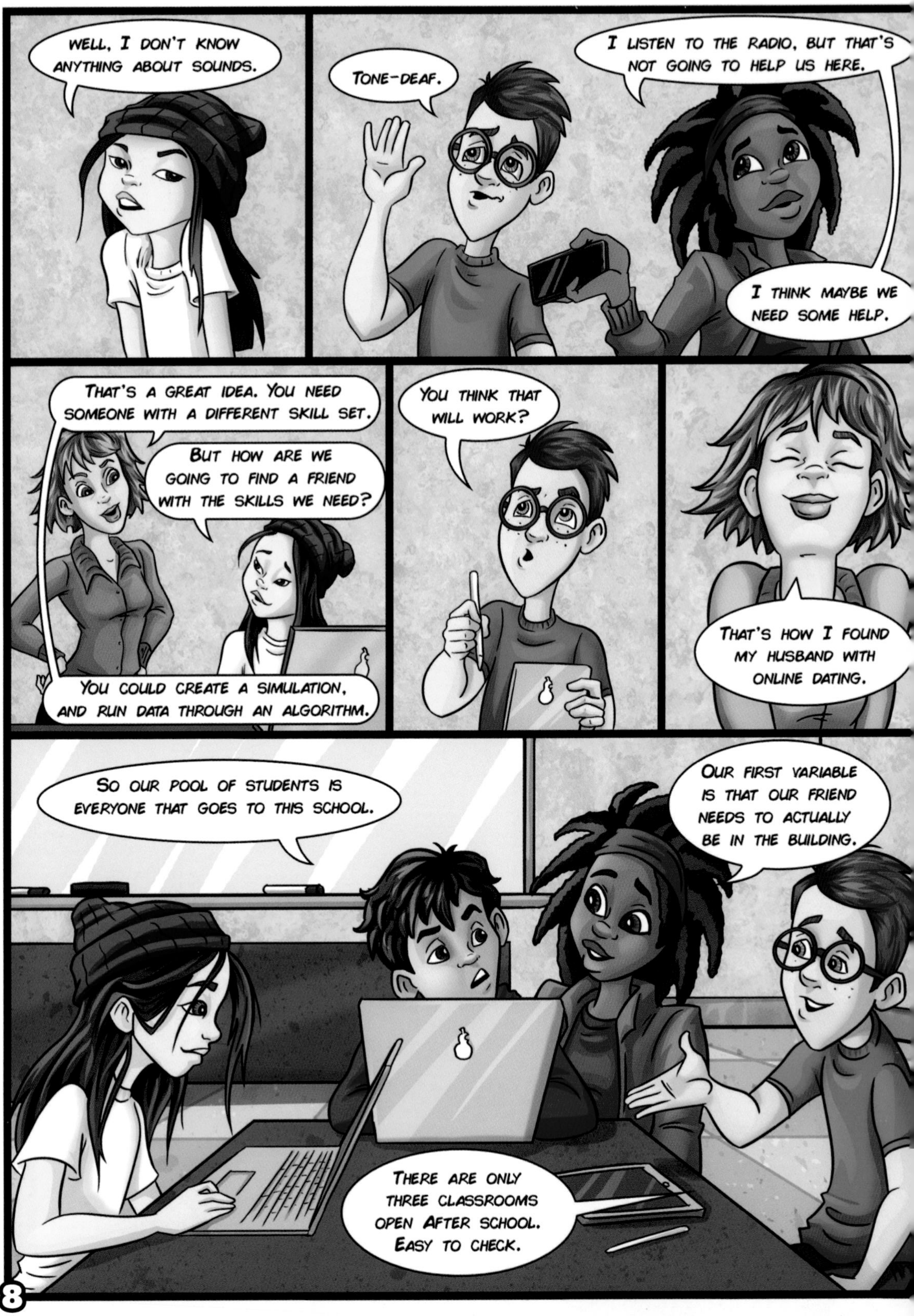
WELL, I DON'T KNOW ANYTHING ABOUT SOUNDS.
TONE-DEAF.
I LISTEN TO THE RADIO, BUT THAT'S NOT GOING TO HELP US HERE.
I THINK MAYBE WE NEED SOME HELP.
THAT'S A GREAT IDEA. YOU NEED SOMEONE WITH A DIFFERENT SKILL SET.
BUT HOW ARE WE GOING TO FIND A FRIEND WITH THE SKILLS WE NEED?
YOU COULD CREATE A SIMULATION, AND RUN DATA THROUGH AN ALGORITHM.
YOU THINK THAT WILL WORK?
THAT'S HOW I FOUND MY HUSBAND WITH ONLINE DATING.
SO OUR POOL OF STUDENTS IS EVERYONE THAT GOES TO THIS SCHOOL.
OUR FIRST VARIABLE IS THAT OUR FRIEND NEEDS TO ACTUALLY BE IN THE BUILDING.
THERE ARE ONLY THREE CLASSROOMS OPEN AFTER SCHOOL. EASY TO CHECK.

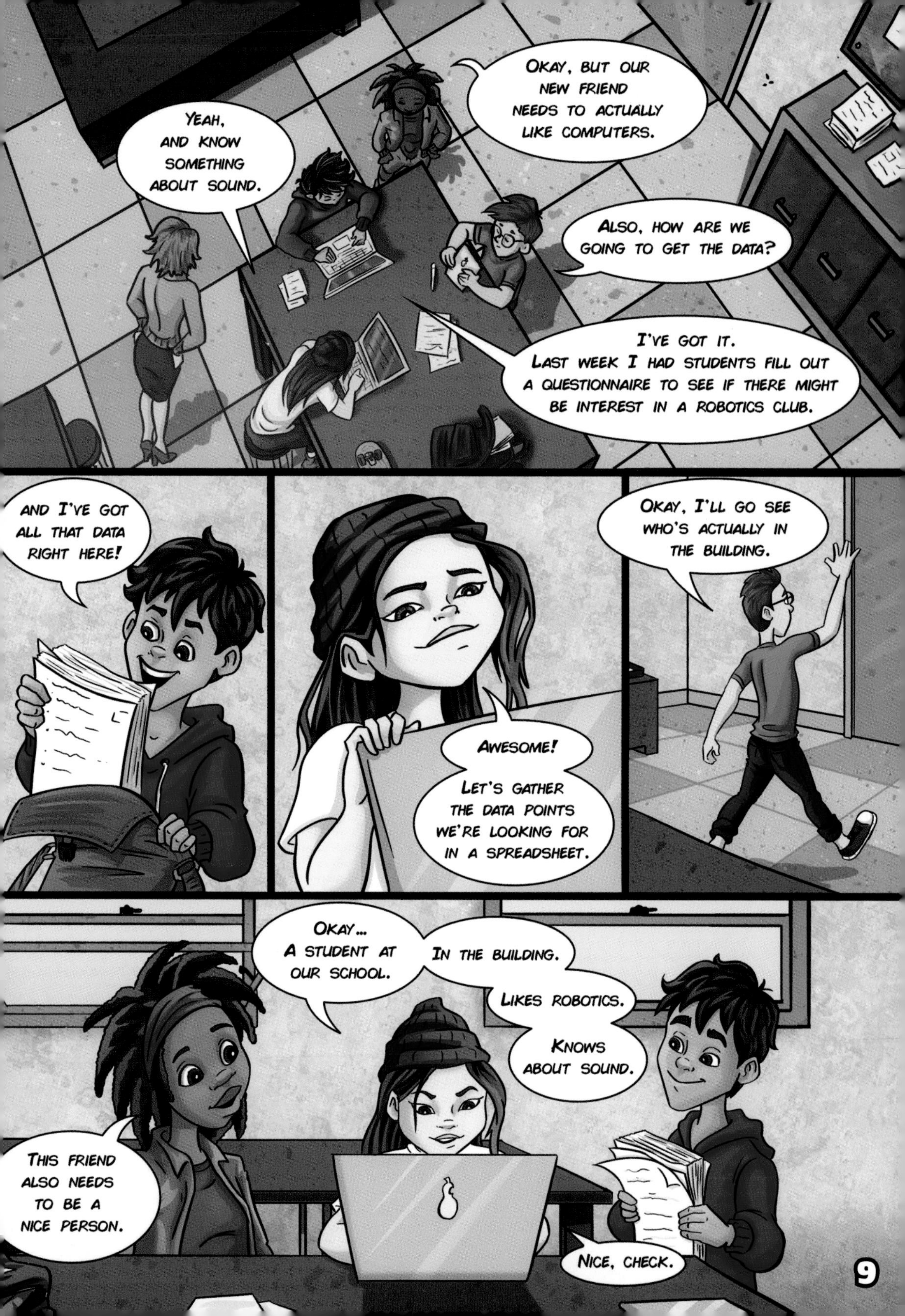
Yeah, and know something about sound.
Okay, but our new friend needs to actually like computers.
Also, how are we going to get the data?
I've got it. Last week I had students fill out a questionnaire to see if there might be interest in a robotics club.
And I've got all that data right here!
Awesome!
Let's gather the data points we're looking for in a spreadsheet.
Okay, I'll go see who's actually in the building.
Okay... A student at our school.
In the building.
Likes robotics.
Knows about sound.
This friend also needs to be a nice person.
Nice, check.

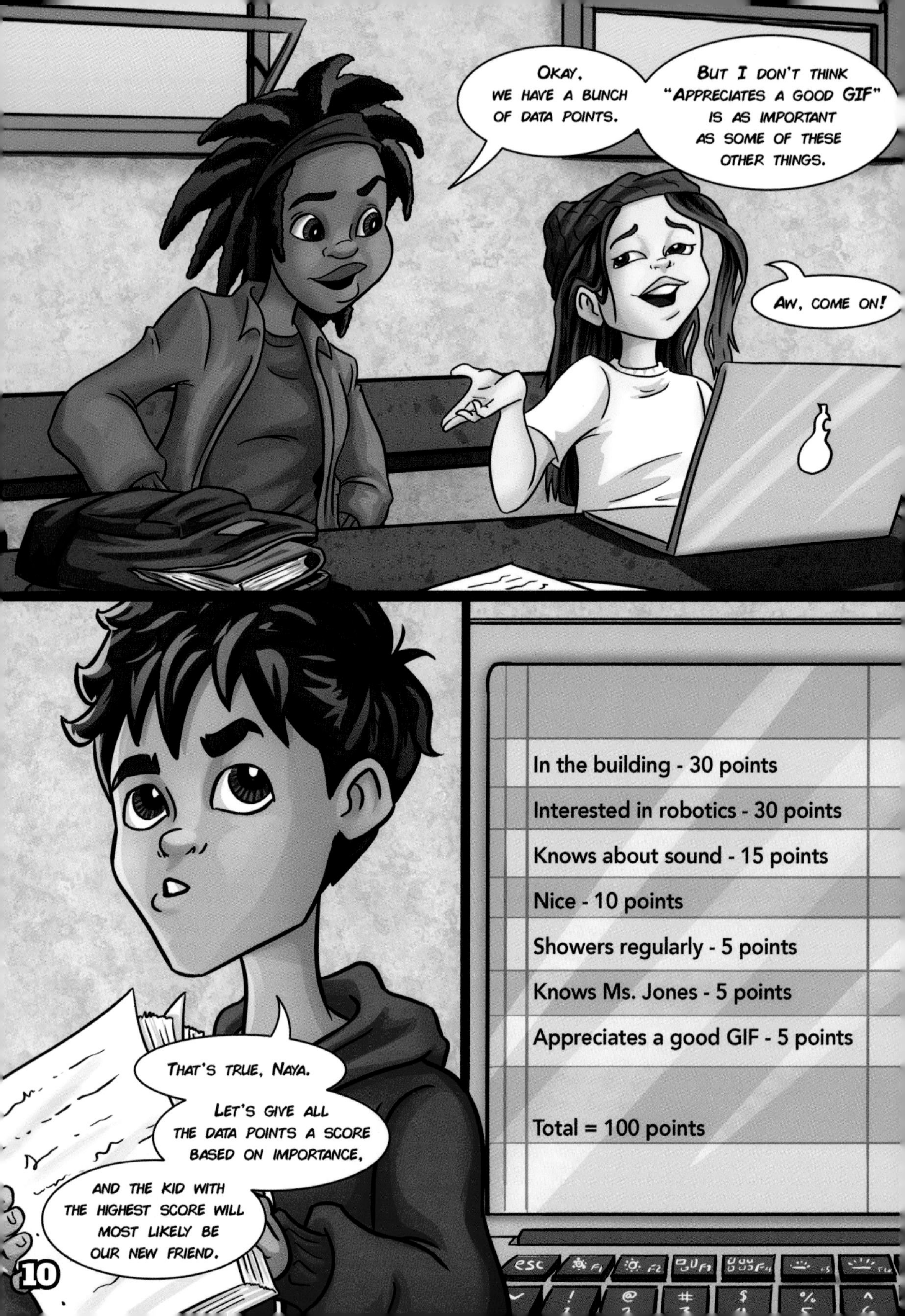

OKAY, WE HAVE A BUNCH OF DATA POINTS.
BUT I DON'T THINK "APPRECIATES A GOOD GIF" IS AS IMPORTANT AS SOME OF THESE OTHER THINGS.
AW, COME ON!
In the building - 30 points
Interested in robotics - 30 points
Knows about sound - 15 points
Nice - 10 points
Showers regularly - 5 points
Knows Ms. Jones - 5 points
Appreciates a good GIF - 5 points
Total = 100 points
THAT'S TRUE, NAYA.
LET'S GIVE ALL THE DATA POINTS A SCORE BASED ON IMPORTANCE,
AND THE KID WITH THE HIGHEST SCORE WILL MOST LIKELY BE OUR NEW FRIEND.

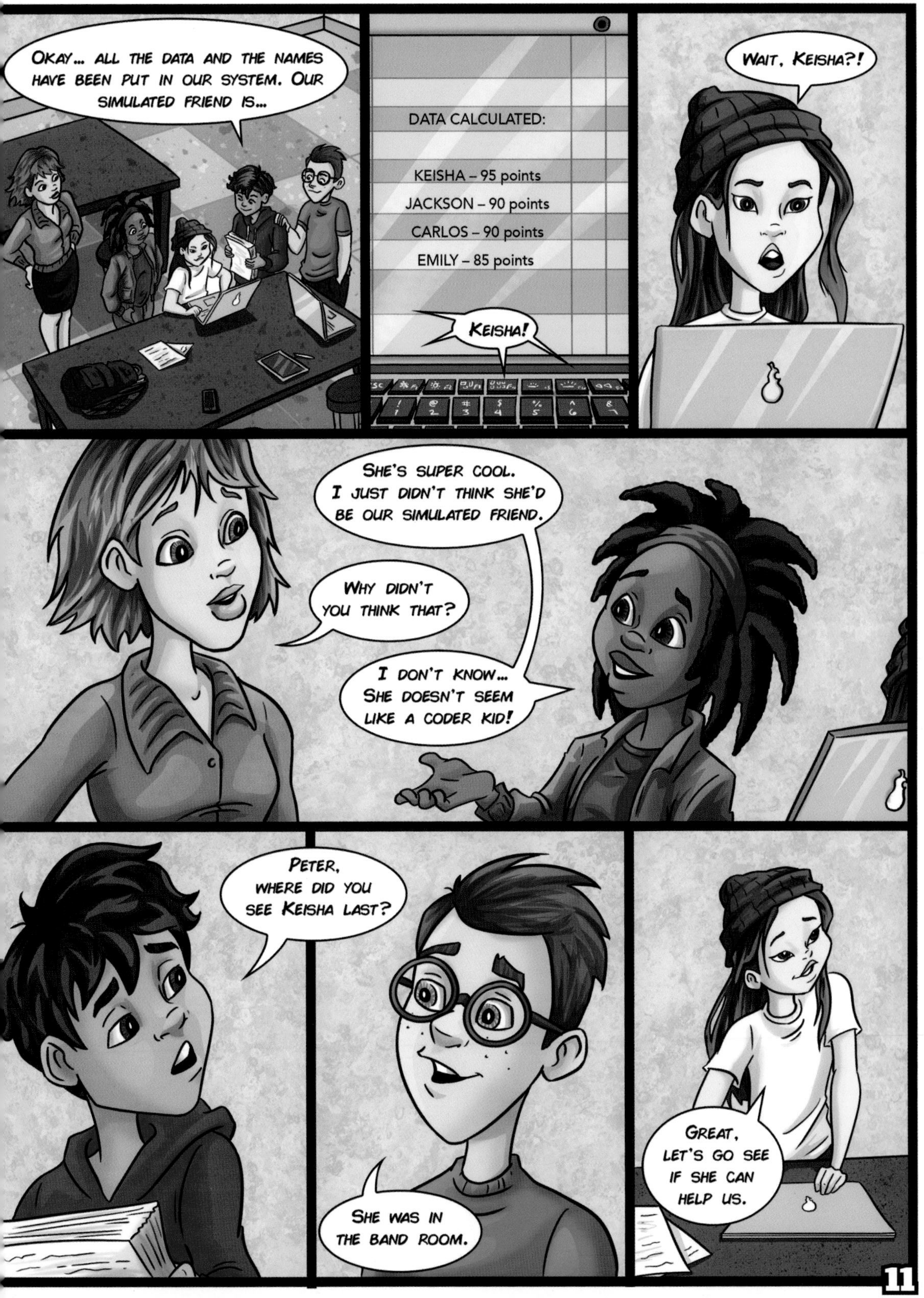

OKAY... ALL THE DATA AND THE NAMES HAVE BEEN PUT IN OUR SYSTEM. OUR SIMULATED FRIEND IS...
DATA CALCULATED:
KEISHA – 95 points
JACKSON – 90 points
CARLOS – 90 points
EMILY – 85 points
KEISHA!
WAIT, KEISHA?!
SHE'S SUPER COOL. I JUST DIDN'T THINK SHE'D BE OUR SIMULATED FRIEND.
WHY DIDN'T YOU THINK THAT?
I DON'T KNOW... SHE DOESN'T SEEM LIKE A CODER KID!
PETER, WHERE DID YOU SEE KEISHA LAST?
SHE WAS IN THE BAND ROOM.
GREAT, LET'S GO SEE IF SHE CAN HELP US.

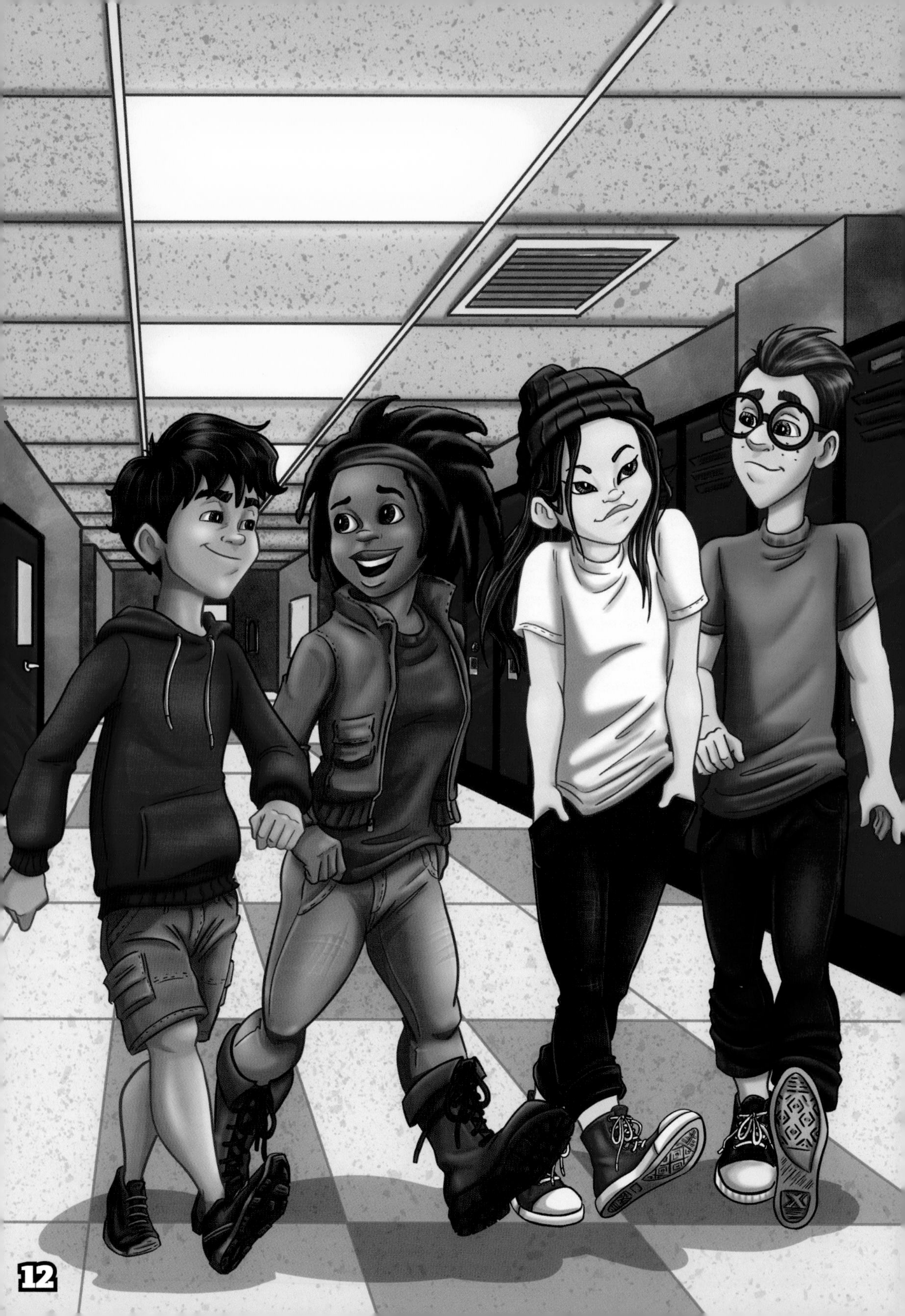

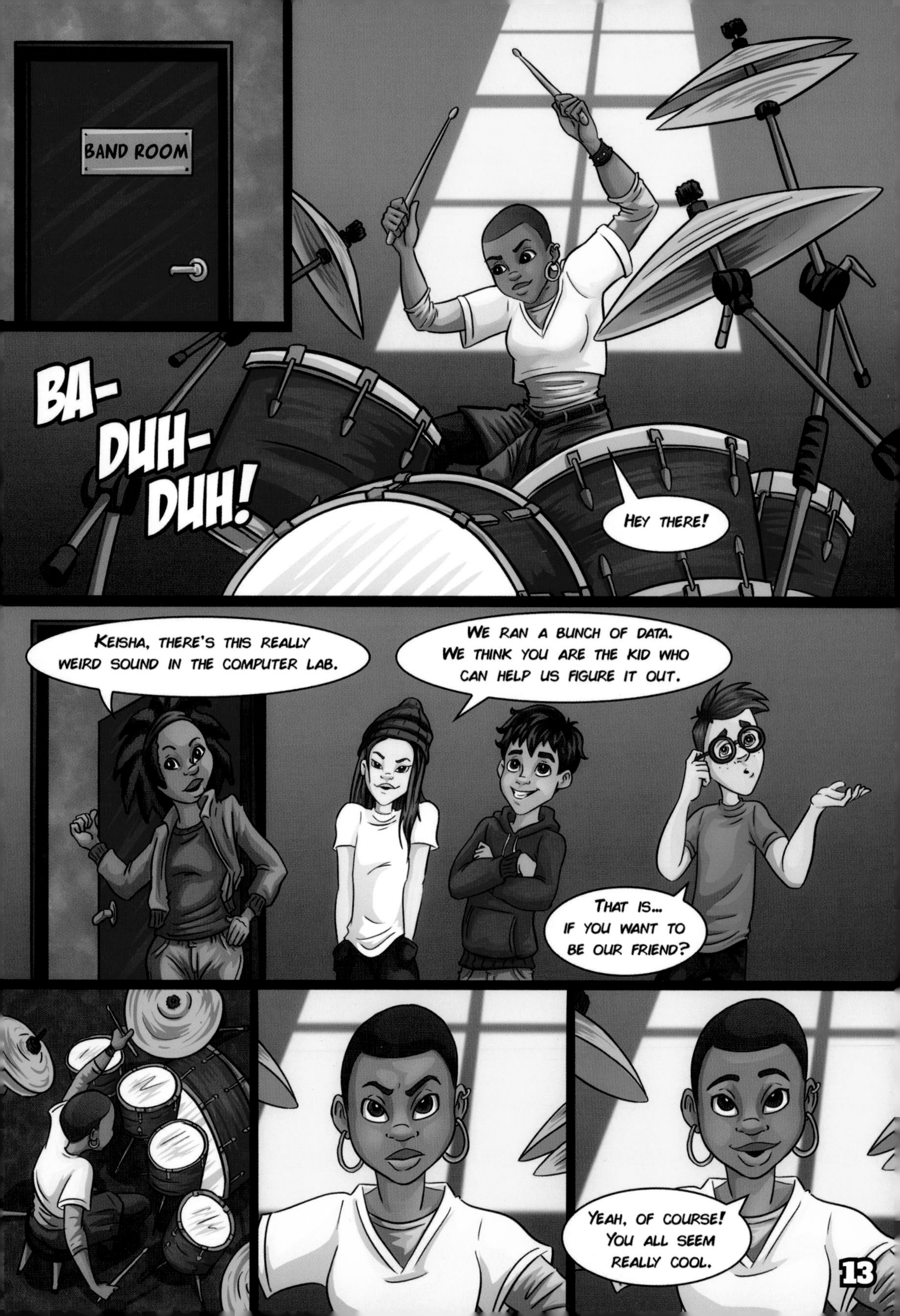
BAND ROOM
BA-DUH-DUH!
HEY THERE!
KEISHA, THERE'S THIS REALLY WEIRD SOUND IN THE COMPUTER LAB.
WE RAN A BUNCH OF DATA. WE THINK YOU ARE THE KID WHO CAN HELP US FIGURE IT OUT.
THAT IS... IF YOU WANT TO BE OUR FRIEND?
YEAH, OF COURSE! YOU ALL SEEM REALLY COOL.

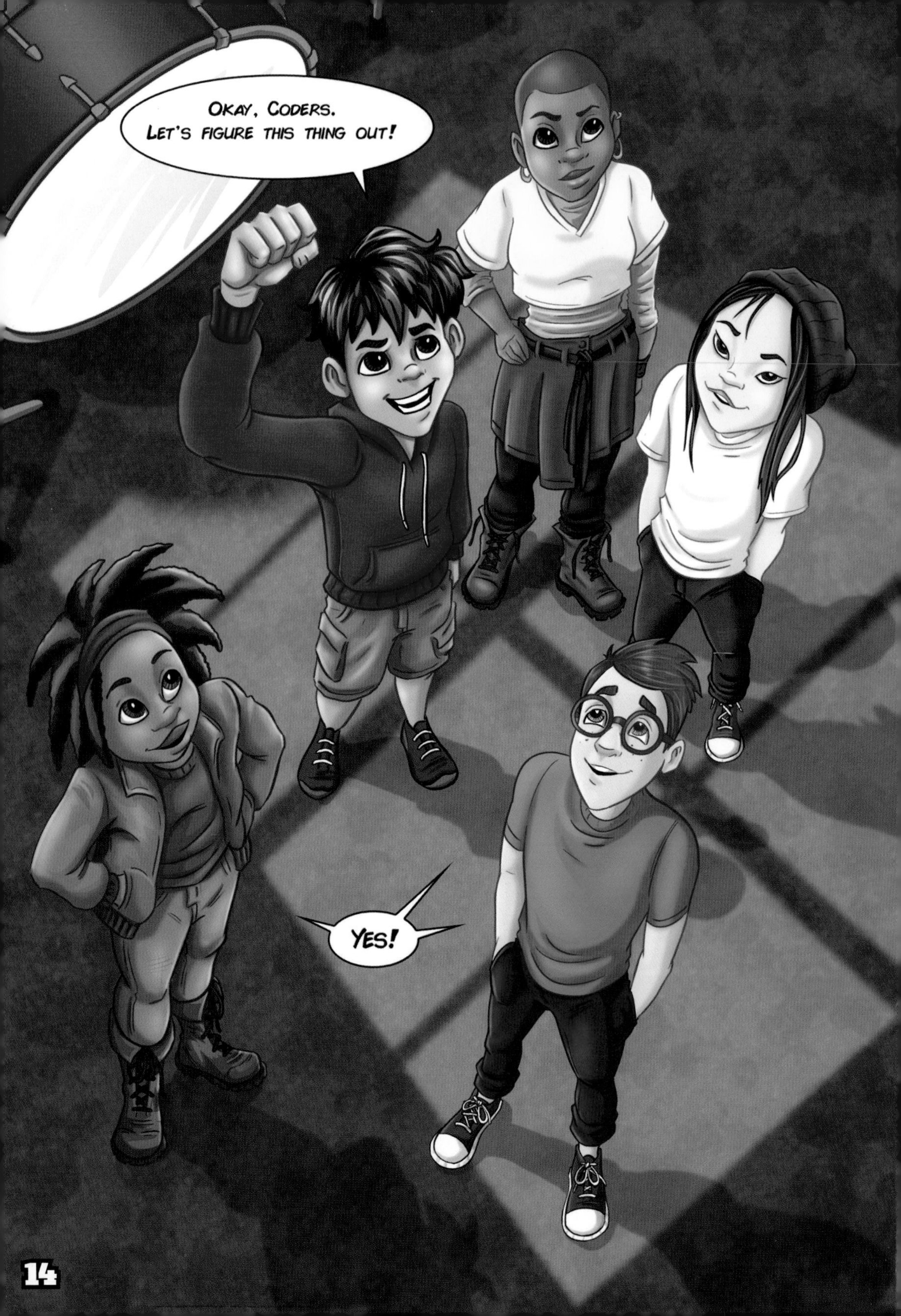
OKAY, CODERS.
LET'S FIGURE THIS THING OUT!
YES!

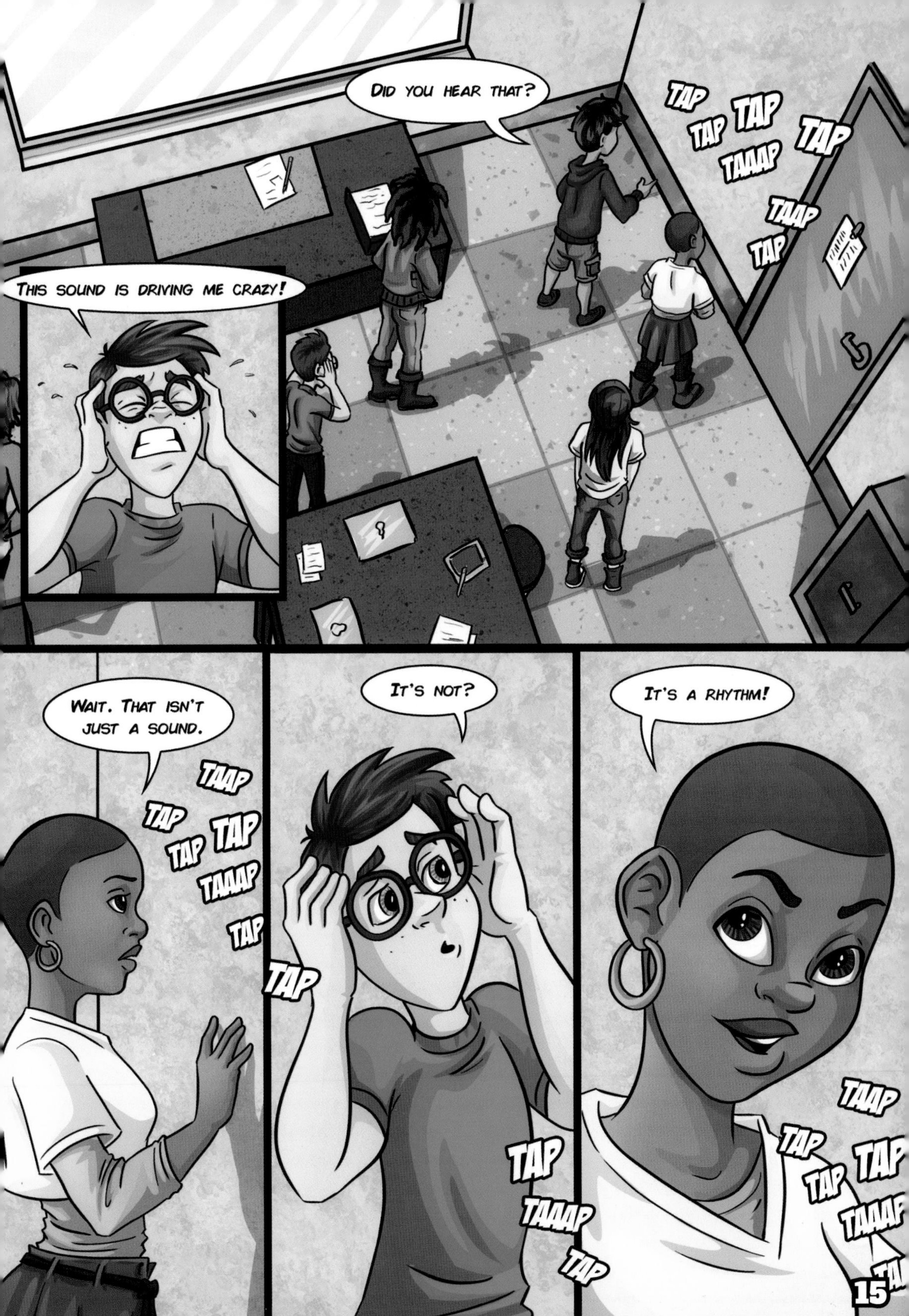
DID YOU HEAR THAT?
TAP
TAP TAP
TAP
TAAAP
TAAP
TAP
THIS SOUND IS DRIVING ME CRAZY!
WAIT. THAT ISN'T JUST A SOUND.
TAAP
TAP
TAP TAP
TAAAP
TAP
TAP
IT'S NOT?
TAP
TAAAP
TAP
IT'S A RHYTHM!
TAAP
TAP
TAP TAP
TAAAP

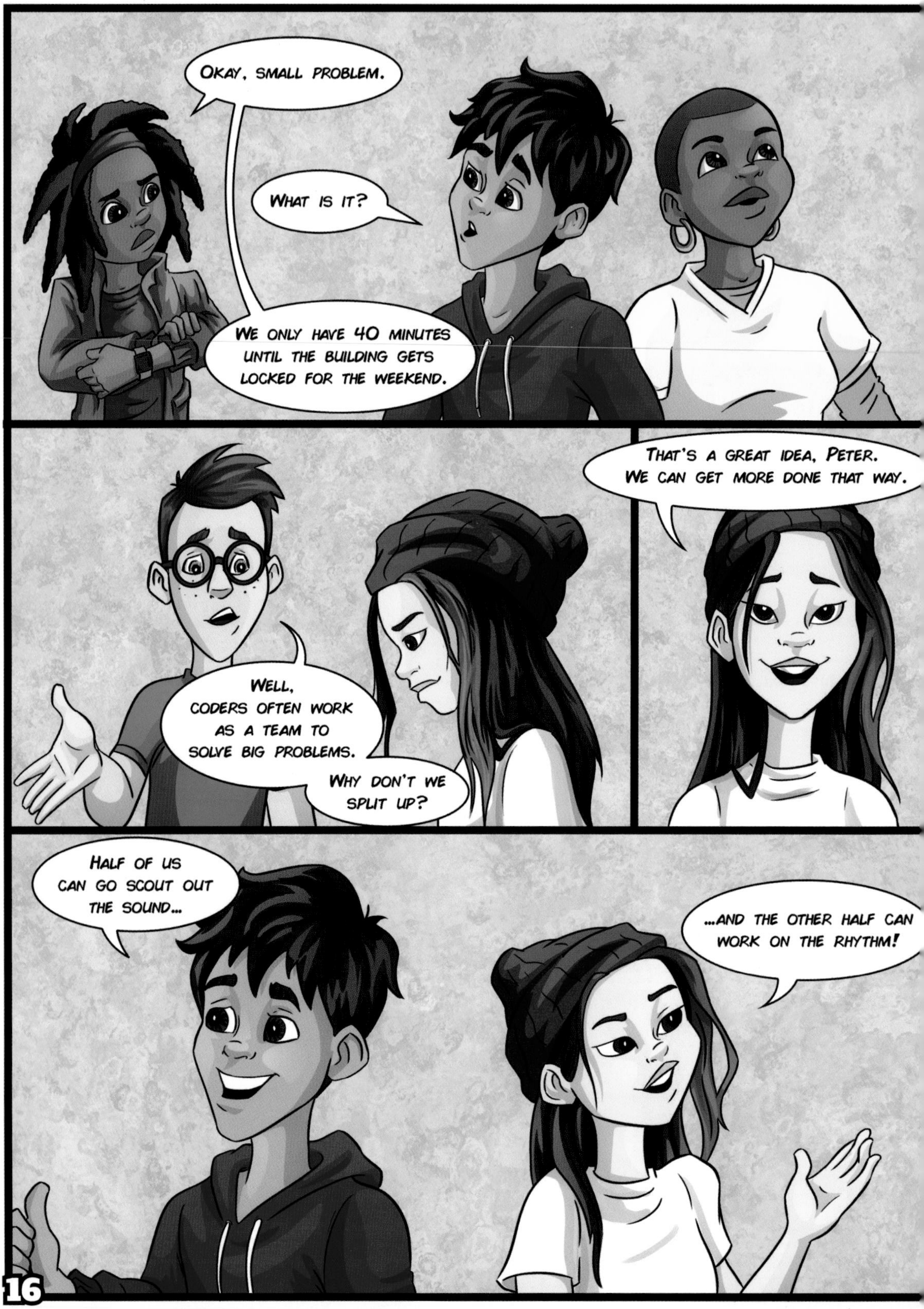
OKAY, SMALL PROBLEM.
WHAT IS IT?
WE ONLY HAVE 40 MINUTES UNTIL THE BUILDING GETS LOCKED FOR THE WEEKEND.
WELL, CODERS OFTEN WORK AS A TEAM TO SOLVE BIG PROBLEMS.
WHY DON'T WE SPLIT UP?
THAT'S A GREAT IDEA, PETER. WE CAN GET MORE DONE THAT WAY.
HALF OF US CAN GO SCOUT OUT THE SOUND...
...AND THE OTHER HALF CAN WORK ON THE RHYTHM!

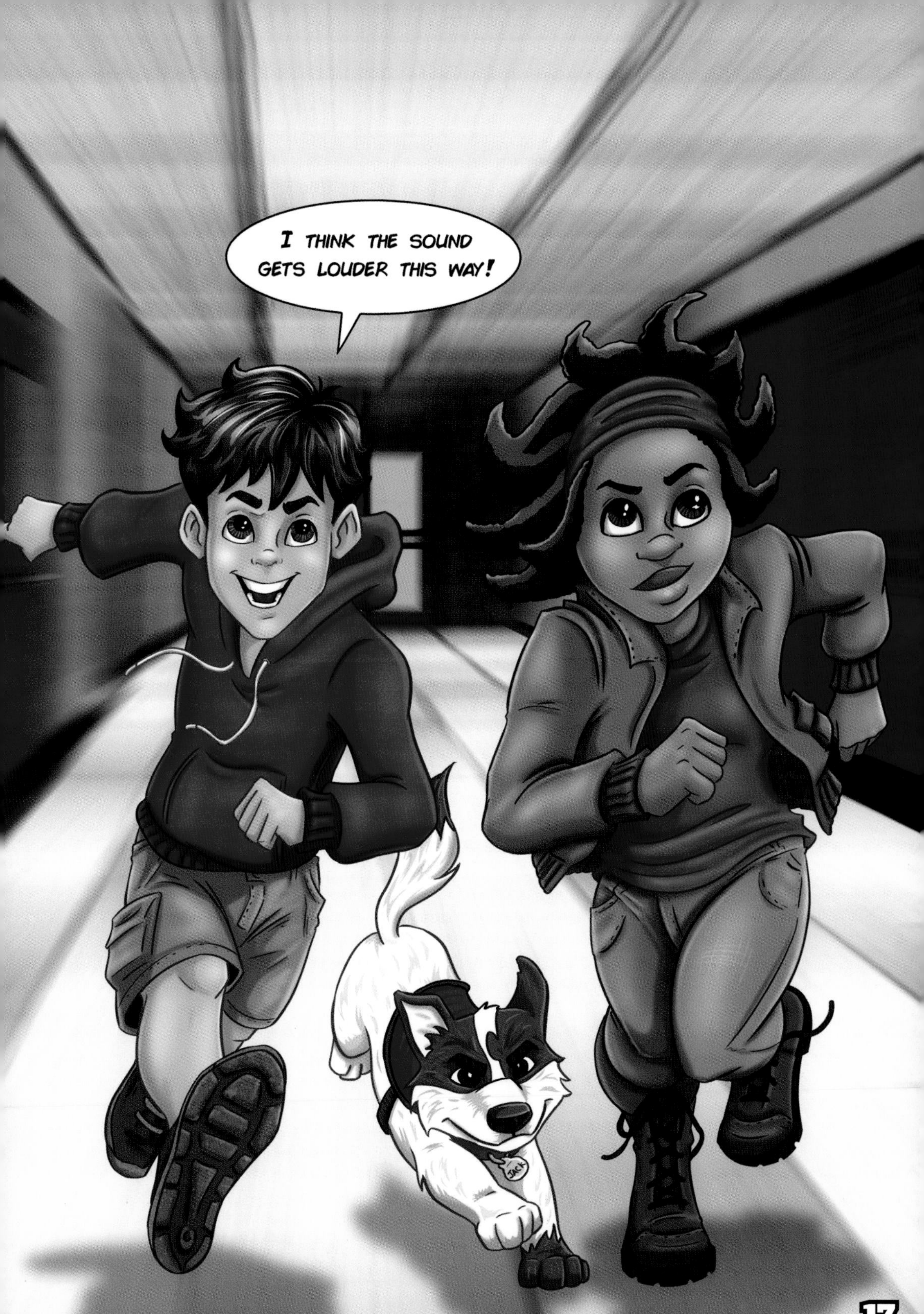
I THINK THE SOUND GETS LOUDER THIS WAY!
JACK

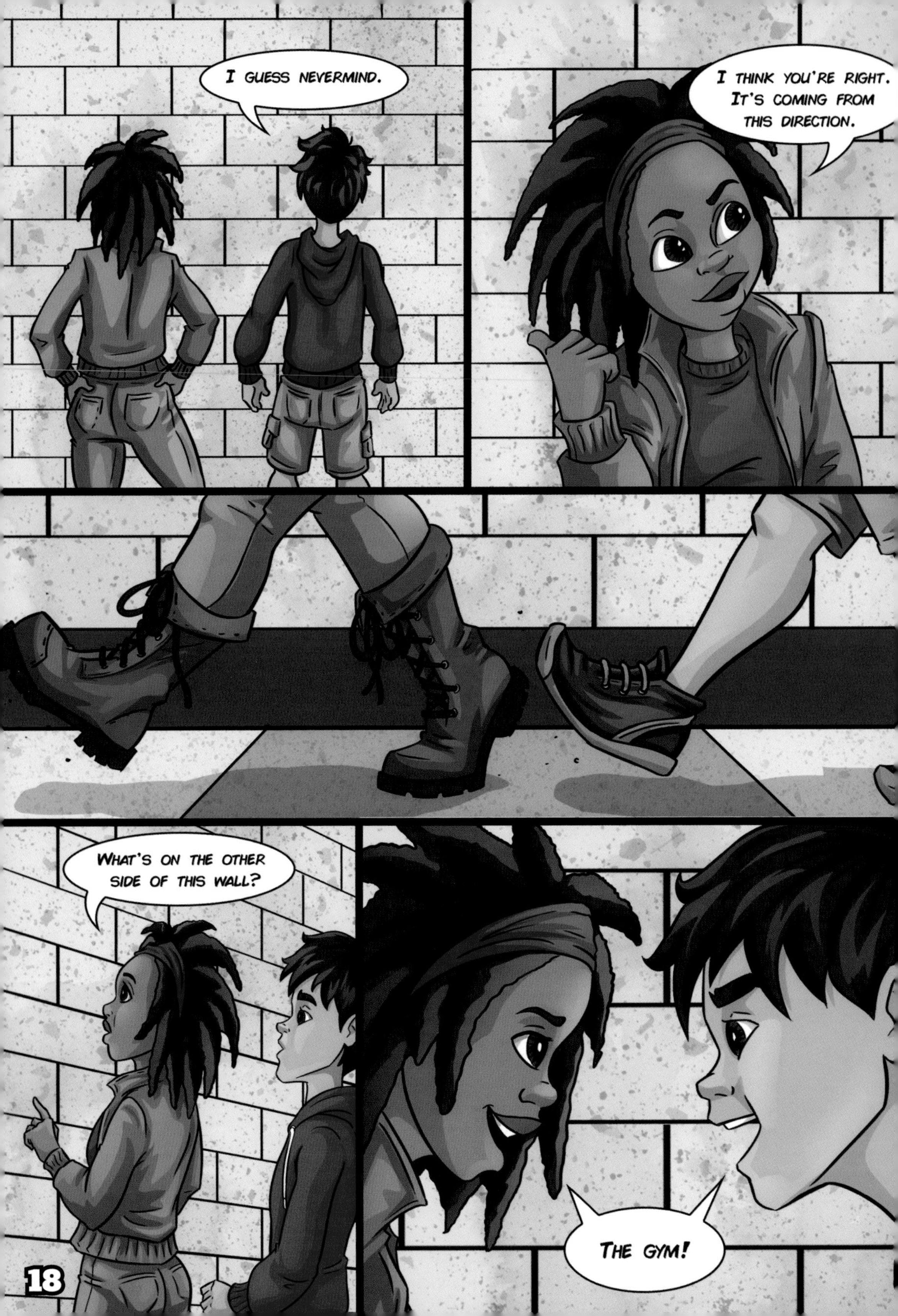
I GUESS NEVERMIND.
I THINK YOU'RE RIGHT. IT'S COMING FROM THIS DIRECTION.
WHAT'S ON THE OTHER SIDE OF THIS WALL?
THE GYM!

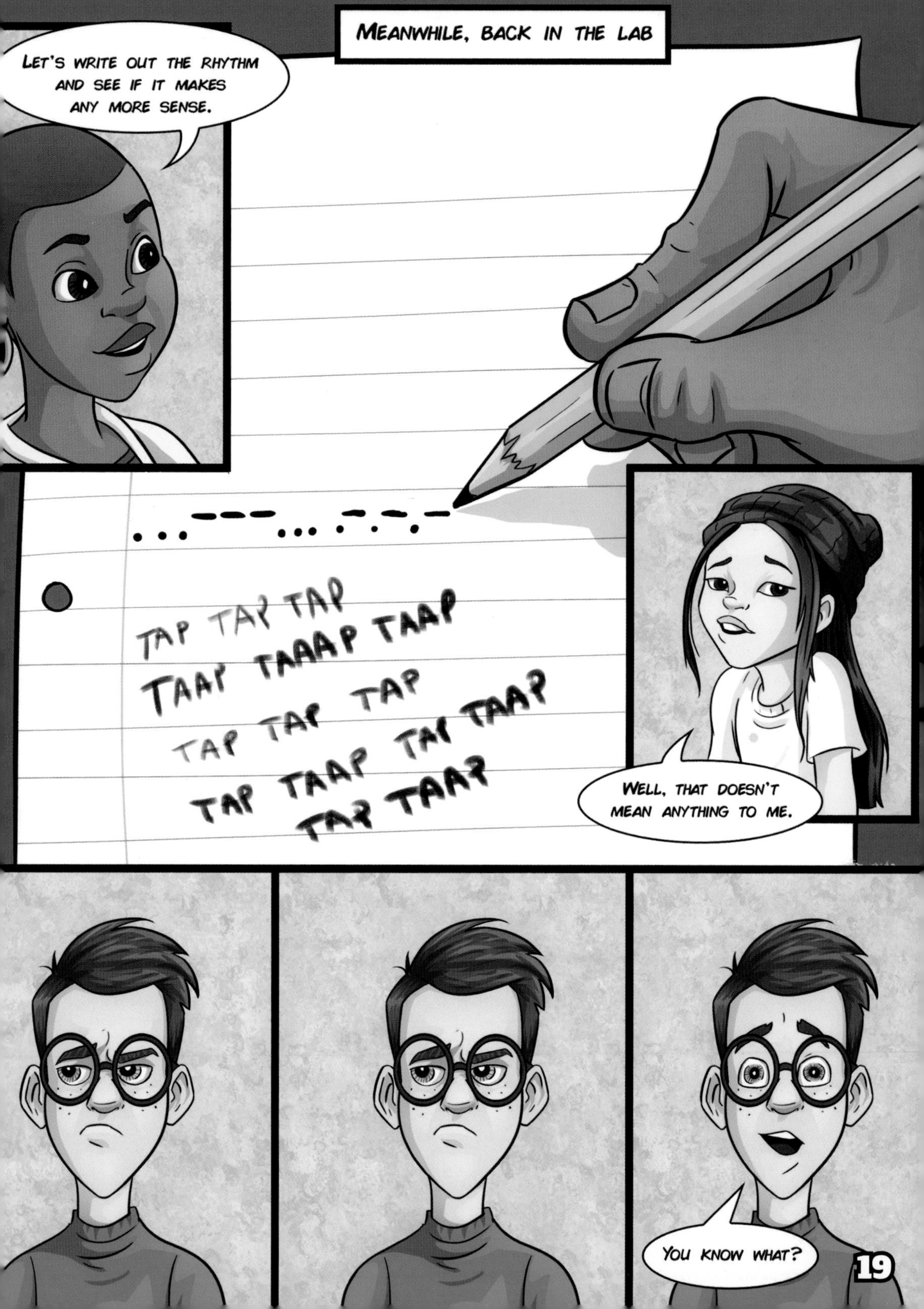
MEANWHILE, BACK IN THE LAB
LET'S WRITE OUT THE RHYTHM AND SEE IF IT MAKES ANY MORE SENSE.
TAP TAP TAP
TAAP TAAAP TAAP
TAP TAP TAP
TAP TAAP TAP TAAP
TAP TAAP
WELL, THAT DOESN'T MEAN ANYTHING TO ME.
YOU KNOW WHAT?

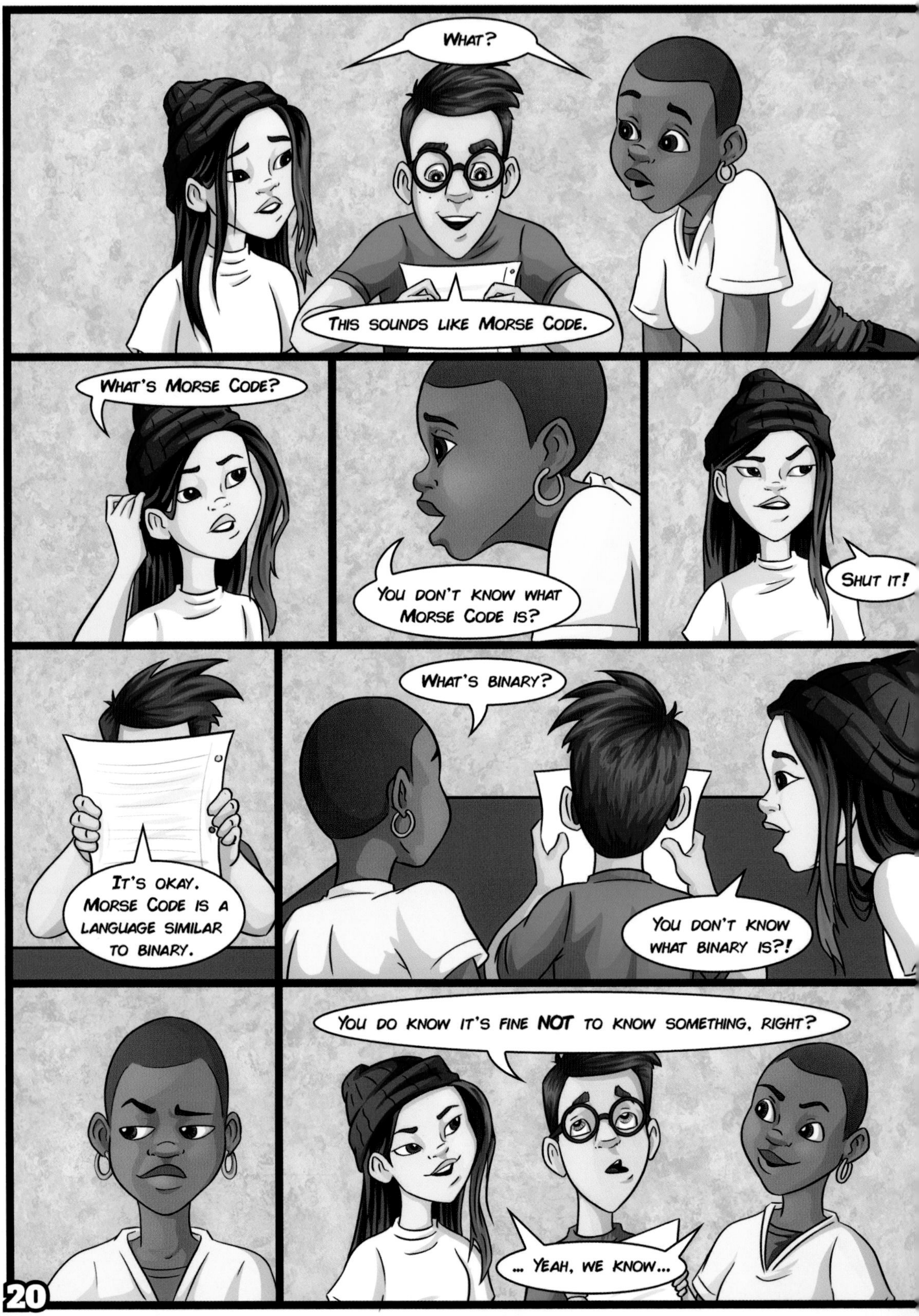
What?
This sounds like Morse Code.
What's Morse Code?
You don't know what Morse Code is?
Shut it!
It's okay. Morse Code is a language similar to binary.
What's binary?
You don't know what binary is?!
You do know it's fine NOT to know something, right?
... Yeah, we know...

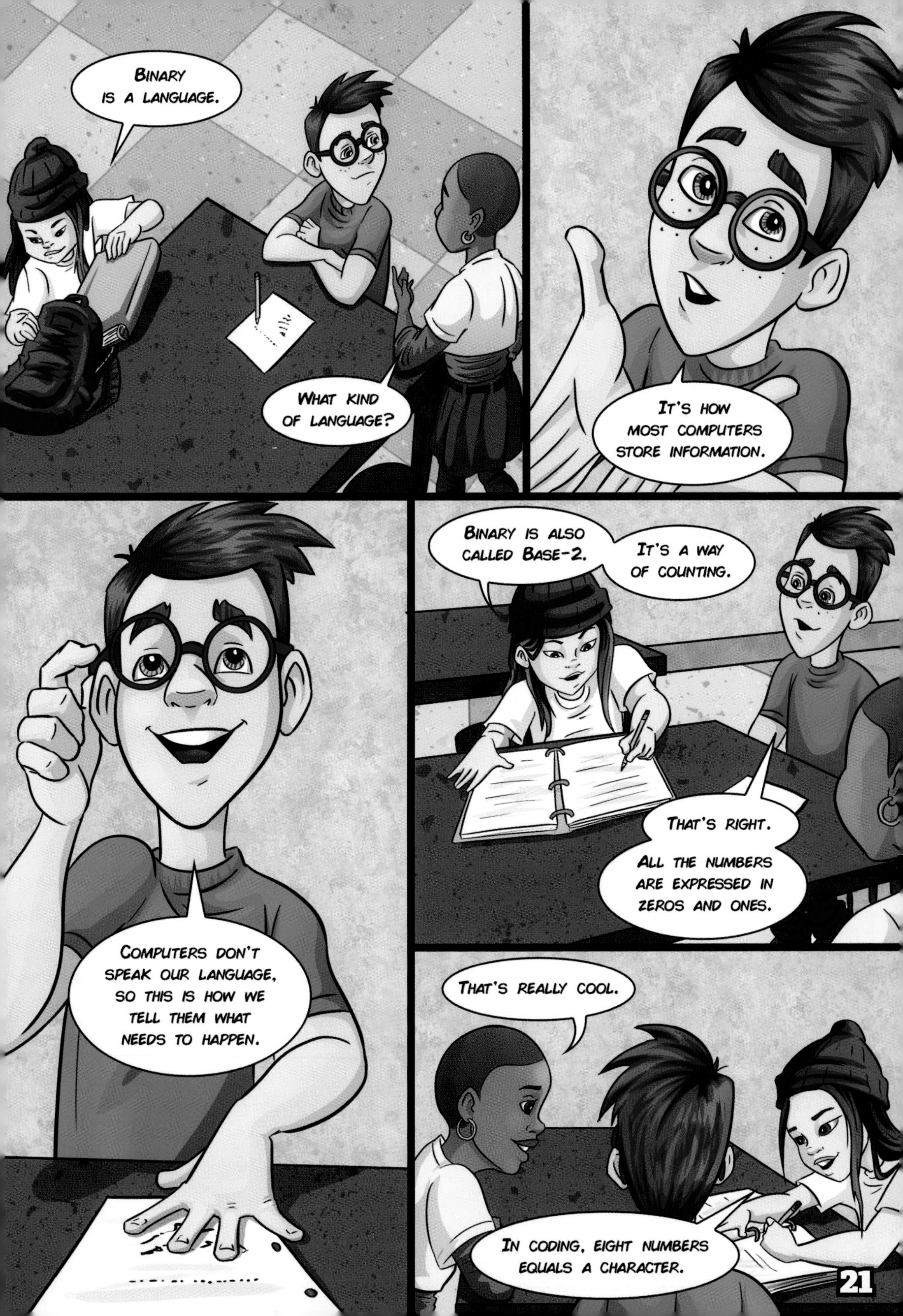

Binary is a language.
What kind of language?
It's how most computers store information.
Computers don't speak our language, so this is how we tell them what needs to happen.
Binary is also called Base-2.
It's a way of counting.
That's right.
All the numbers are expressed in zeros and ones.
That's really cool.
In coding, eight numbers equals a character.

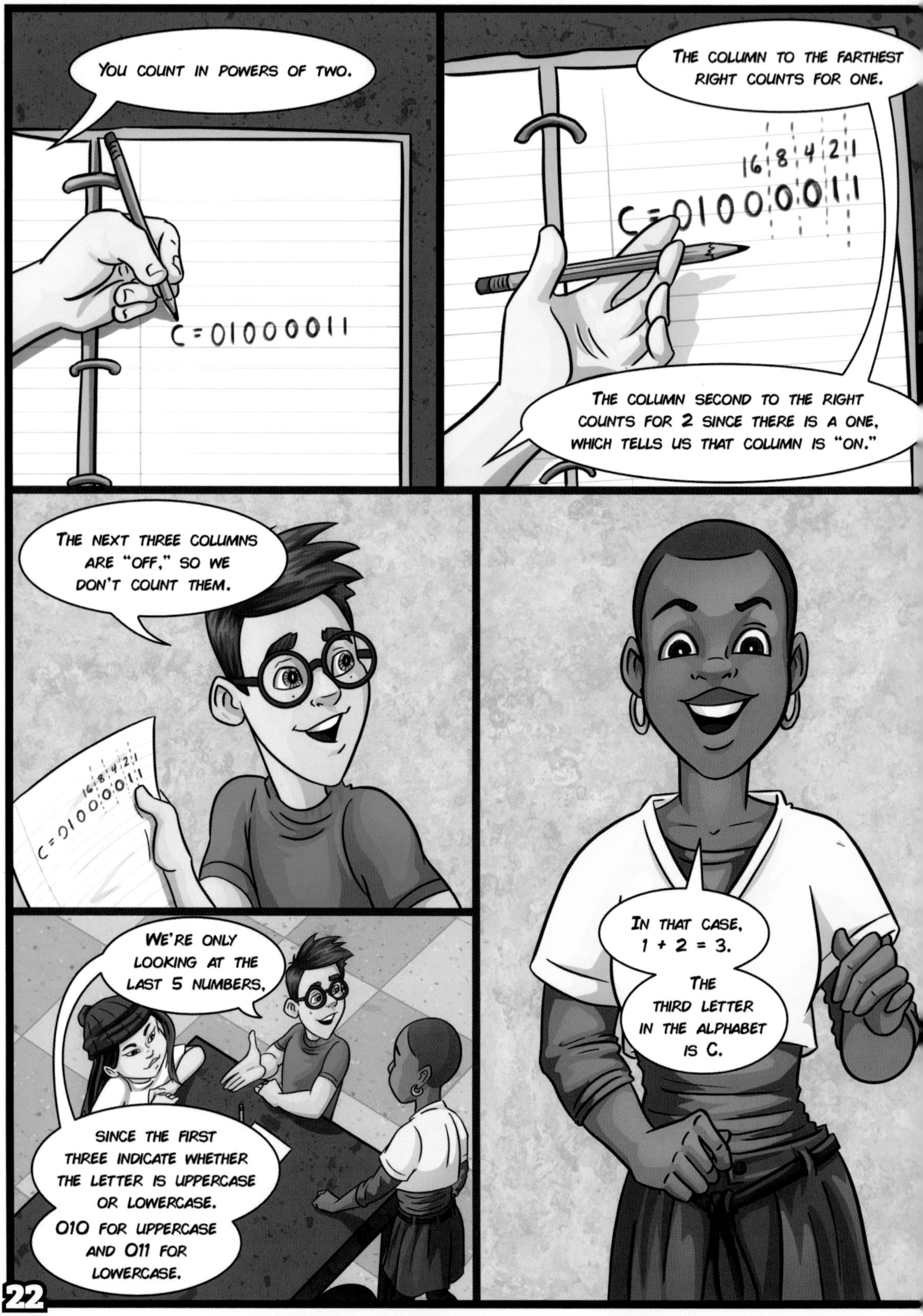

YOU COUNT IN POWERS OF TWO.
C=01000011
THE COLUMN TO THE FARTHEST RIGHT COUNTS FOR ONE.
16 8 4 2 1
C=01000011
THE COLUMN SECOND TO THE RIGHT COUNTS FOR 2 SINCE THERE IS A ONE, WHICH TELLS US THAT COLUMN IS "ON."
THE NEXT THREE COLUMNS ARE "OFF," SO WE DON'T COUNT THEM.
IN THAT CASE, 1 + 2 = 3.
THE THIRD LETTER IN THE ALPHABET IS C.
WE'RE ONLY LOOKING AT THE LAST 5 NUMBERS,
SINCE THE FIRST THREE INDICATE WHETHER THE LETTER IS UPPERCASE OR LOWERCASE.
010 FOR UPPERCASE AND 011 FOR LOWERCASE.

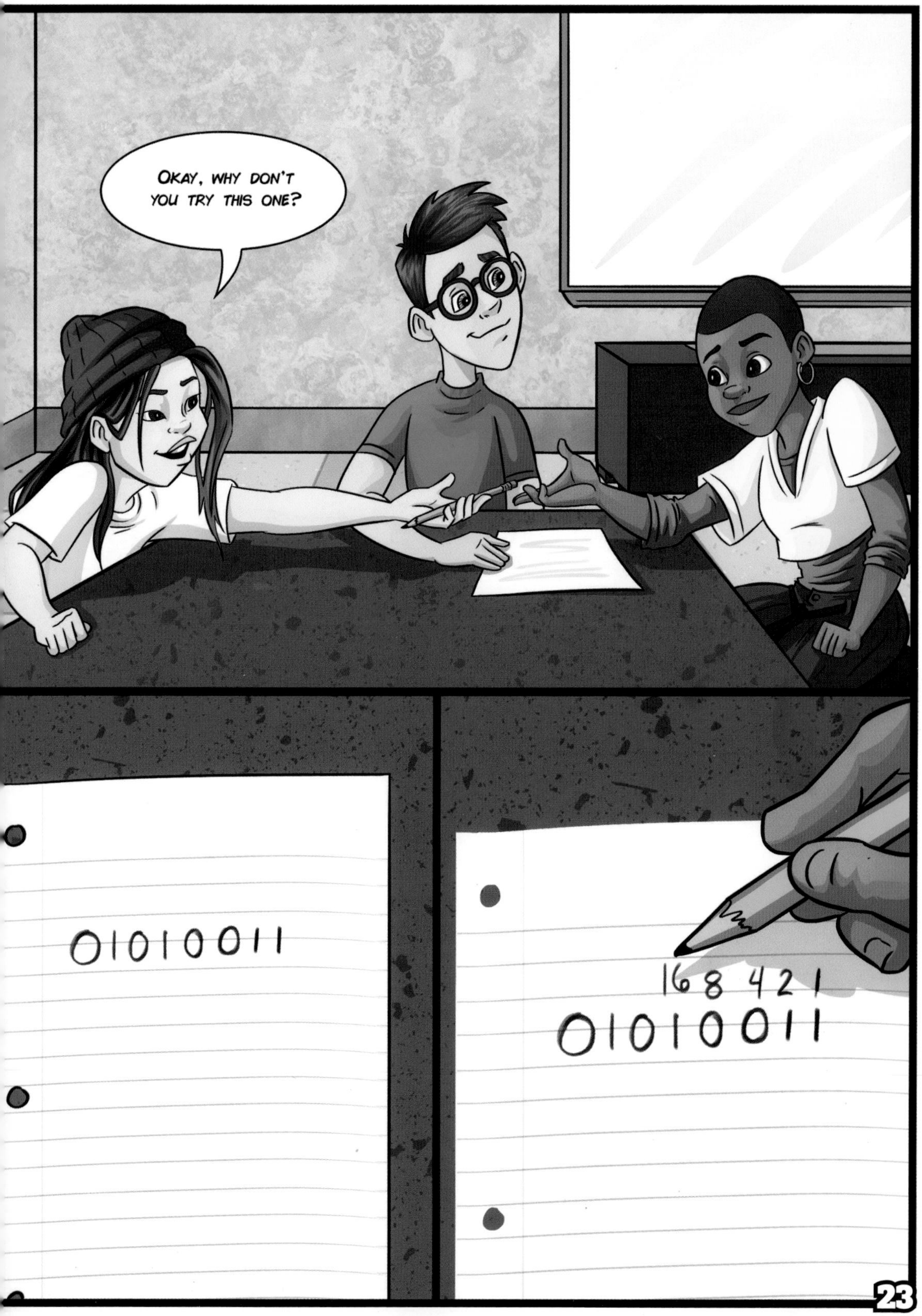
OKAY, WHY DON'T YOU TRY THIS ONE?
01010011
16 8 4 2 1
01010011

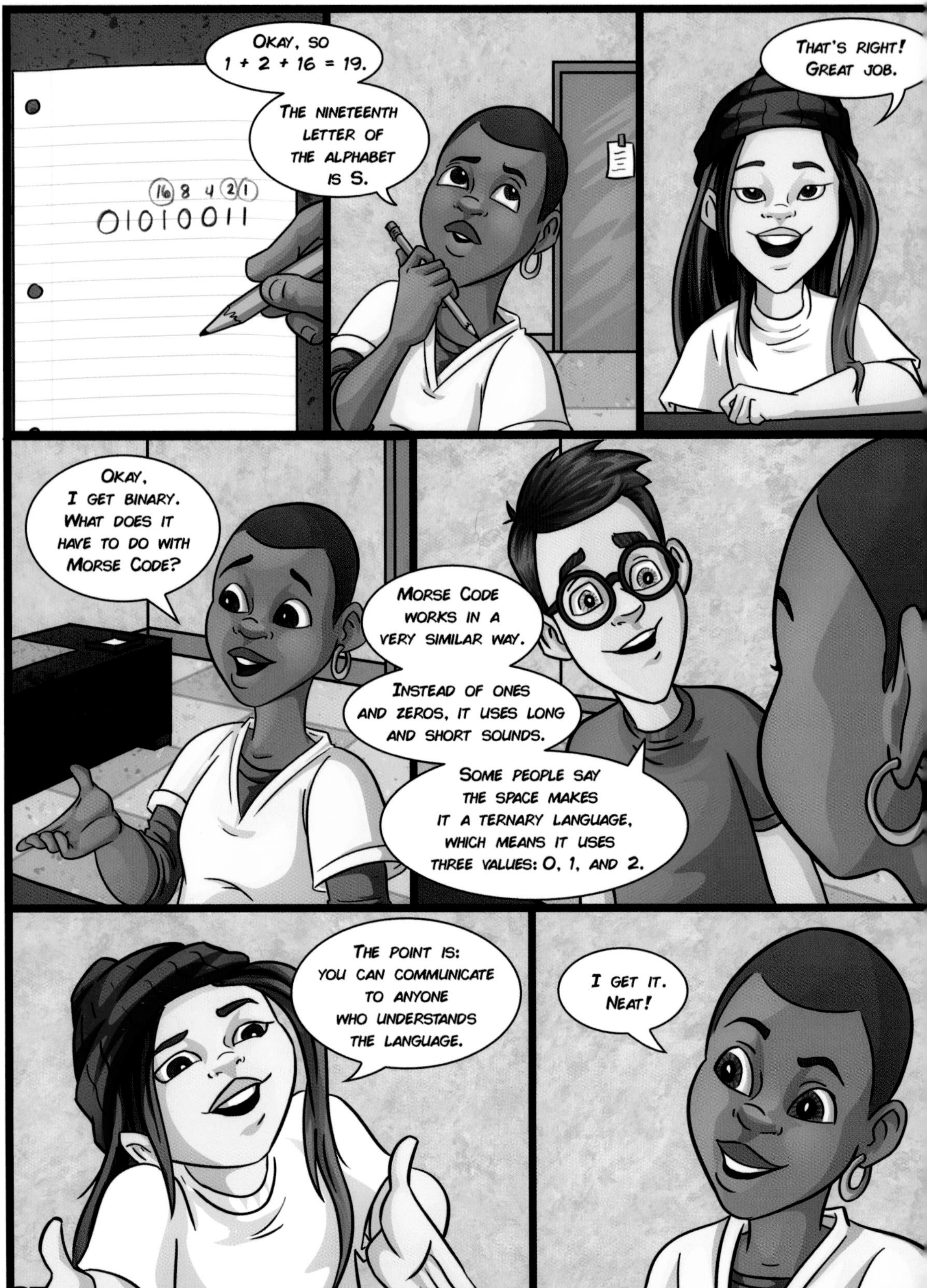
16 8 4 2 1
01010011
Okay, so 1 + 2 + 16 = 19.
The nineteenth letter of the alphabet is S.
That's right! Great job.
Okay, I get binary. What does it have to do with Morse Code?
Morse Code works in a very similar way.
Instead of ones and zeros, it uses long and short sounds.
Some people say the space makes it a ternary language, which means it uses three values: 0, 1, and 2.
The point is: you can communicate to anyone who understands the language.
I get it. Neat!

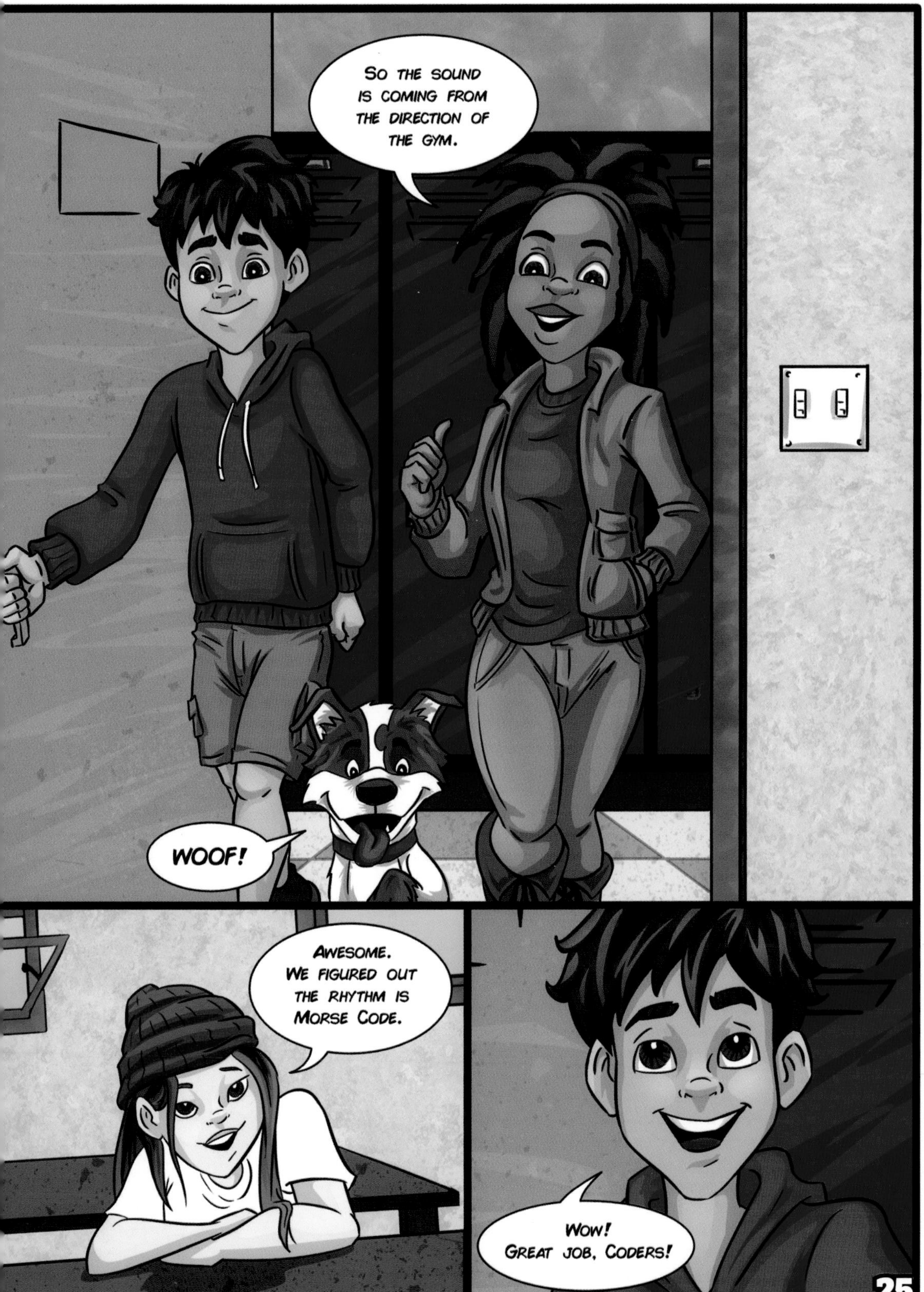

SO THE SOUND IS COMING FROM THE DIRECTION OF THE GYM.
WOOF!
AWESOME. WE FIGURED OUT THE RHYTHM IS MORSE CODE.
WOW! GREAT JOB, CODERS!

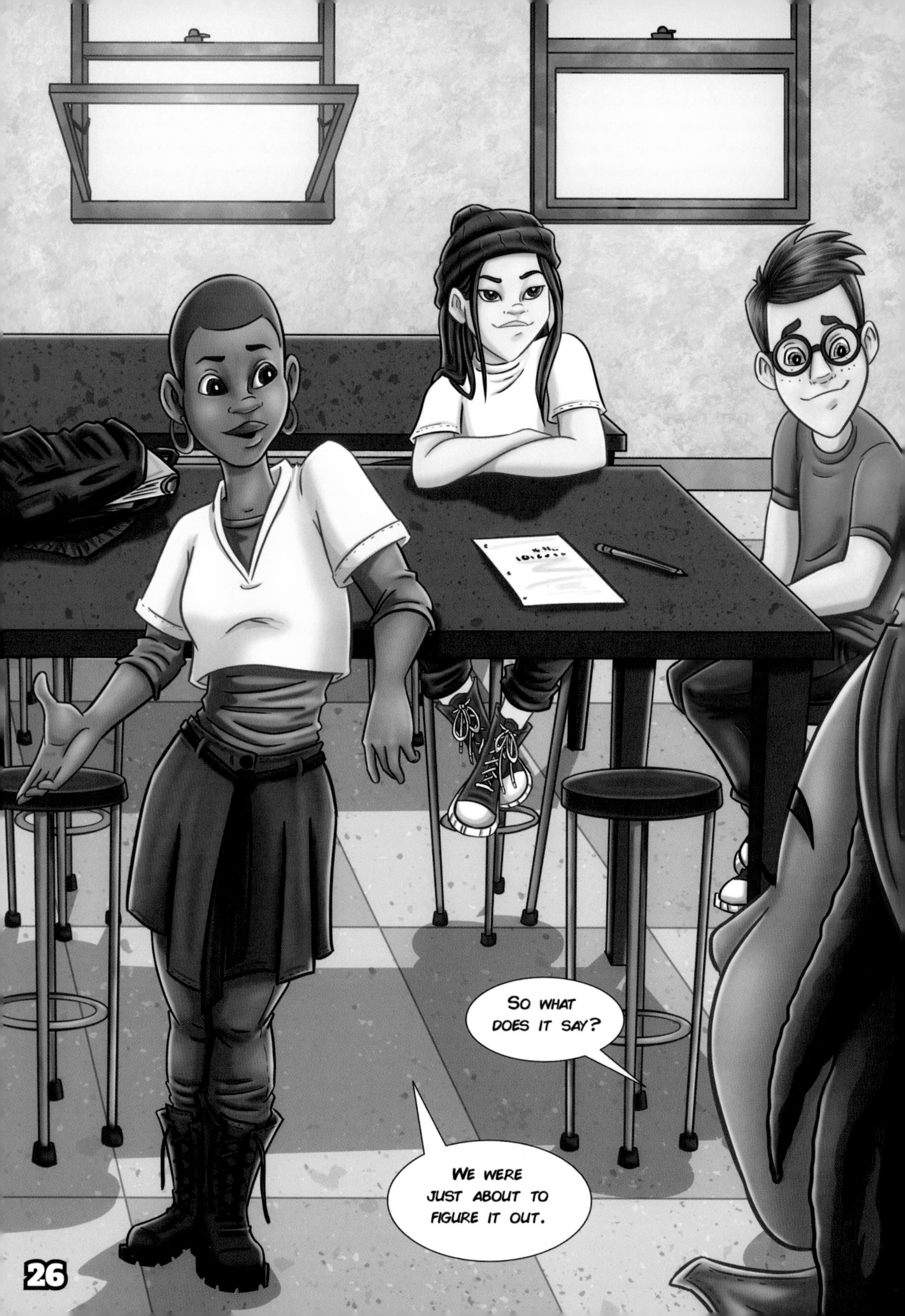
So what does it say?
We were just about to figure it out.

A ●-   J ●---   S ●●●
B -●●●   K -●-   T -
C -●-●   L ●-●●   U ●●-
D -●●   M --   V ●●●-
E ●   N -●   W ●--
F ●●-●   O ---   X -●●-
G --●   P ●--●   Y -●--
H ●●●●   Q --●-   Z --●●
I ●●   R ●-●

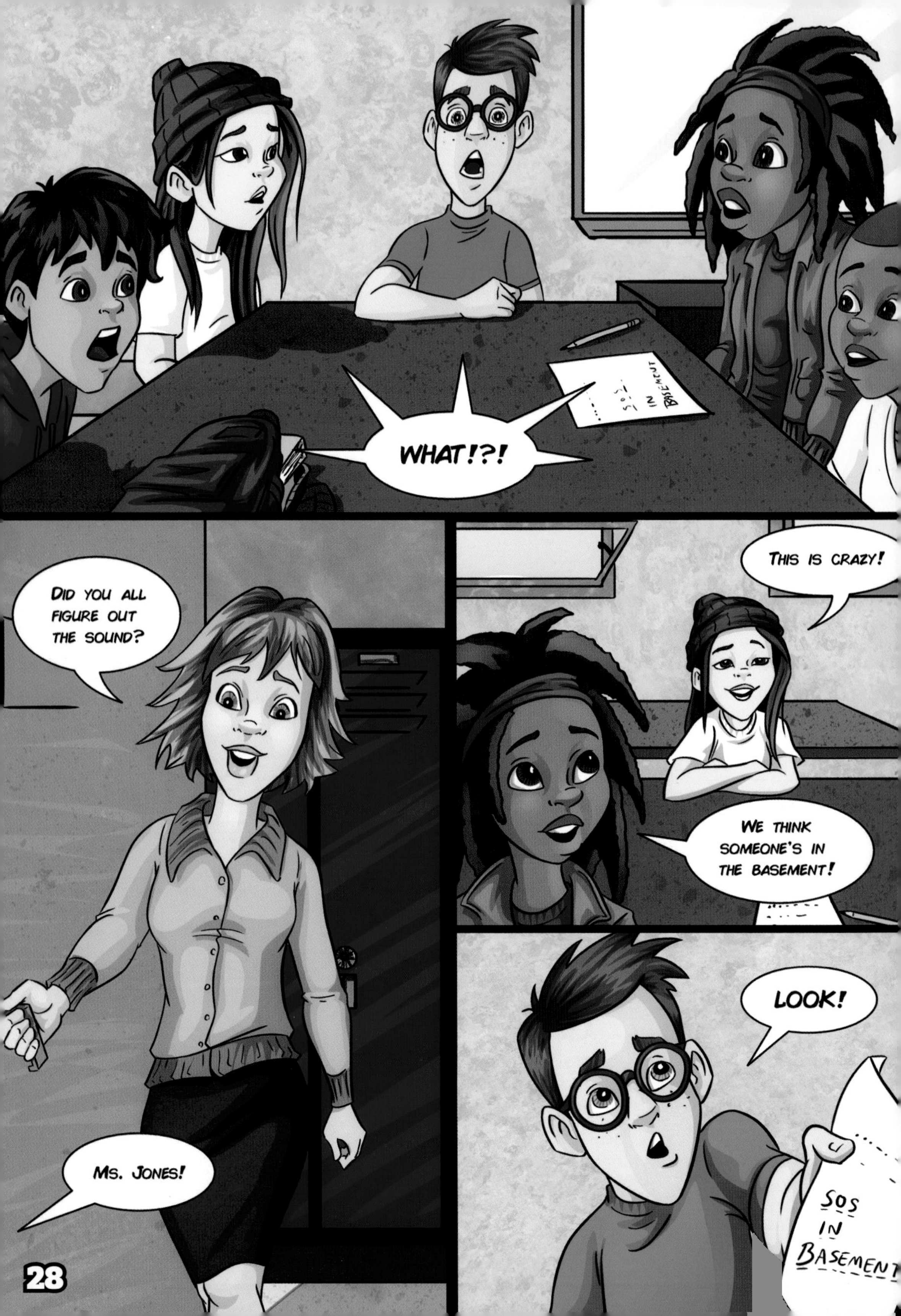

WHAT!?!
DID YOU ALL FIGURE OUT THE SOUND?
MS. JONES!
THIS IS CRAZY!
WE THINK SOMEONE'S IN THE BASEMENT!
LOOK!
SOS IN BASEMENT

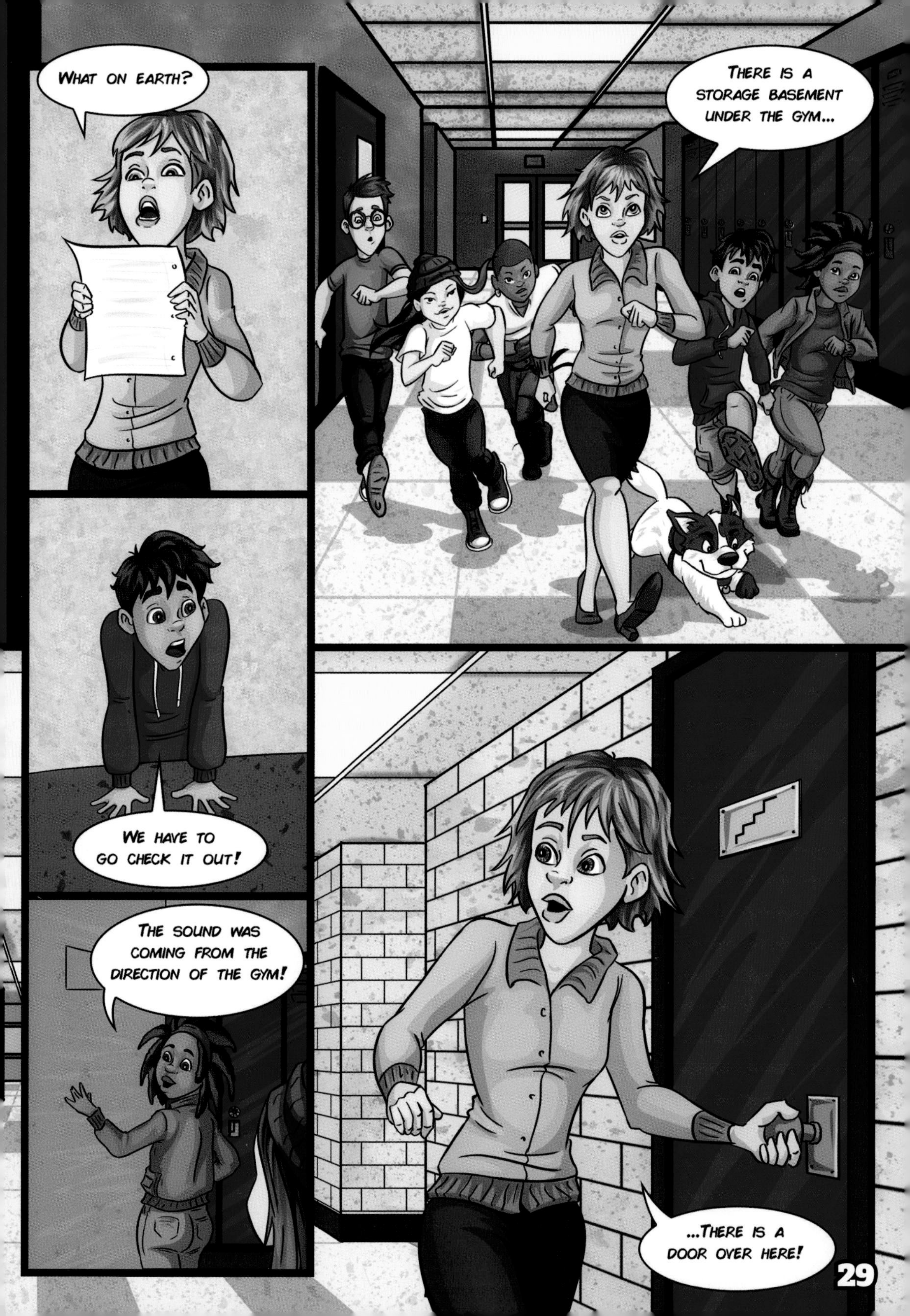
WHAT ON EARTH?
THERE IS A STORAGE BASEMENT UNDER THE GYM...
WE HAVE TO GO CHECK IT OUT!
THE SOUND WAS COMING FROM THE DIRECTION OF THE GYM!
...THERE IS A DOOR OVER HERE!

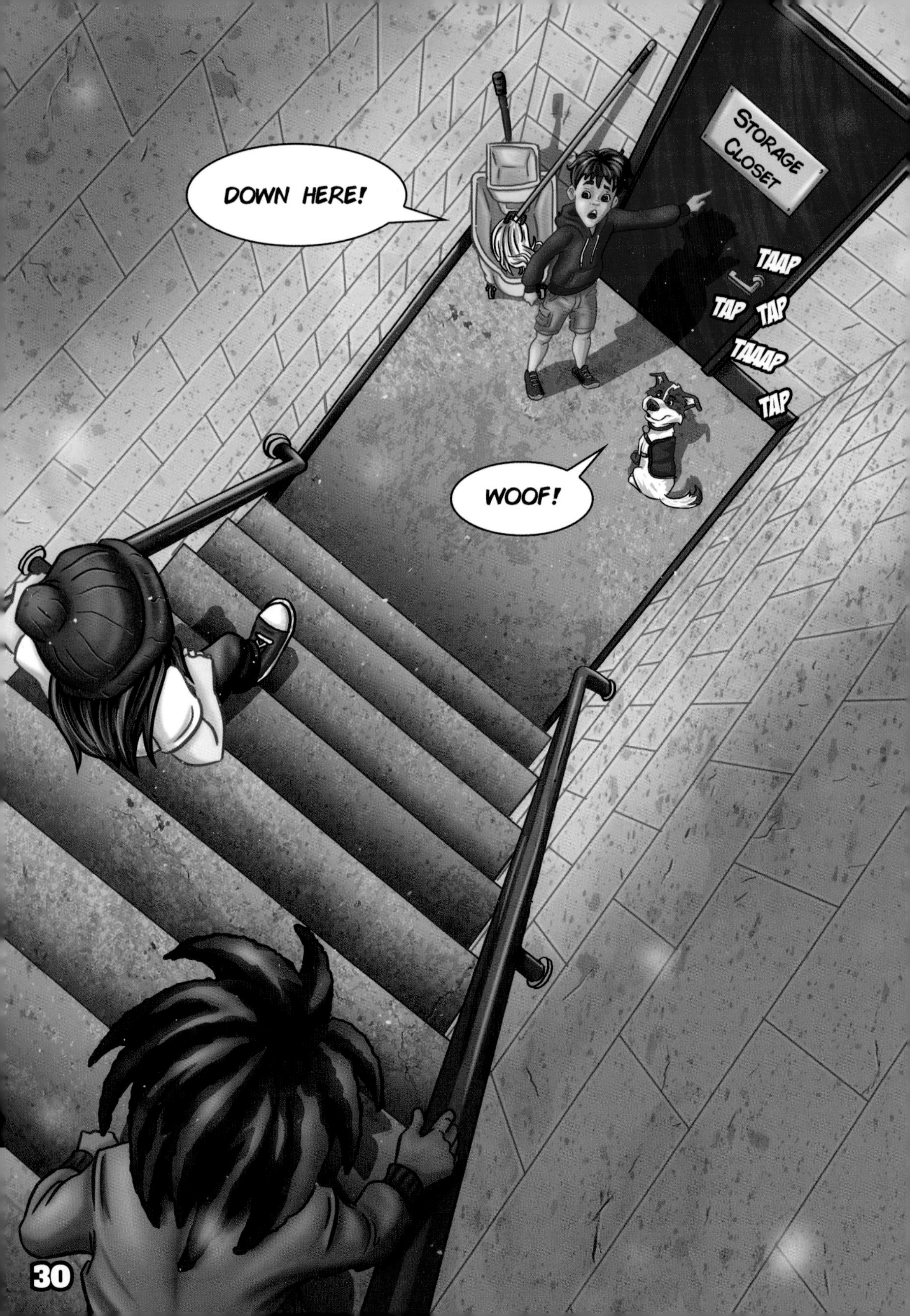
DOWN HERE!
STORAGE CLOSET
TAAP
TAP
TAP
TAAAP
TAP
WOOF!

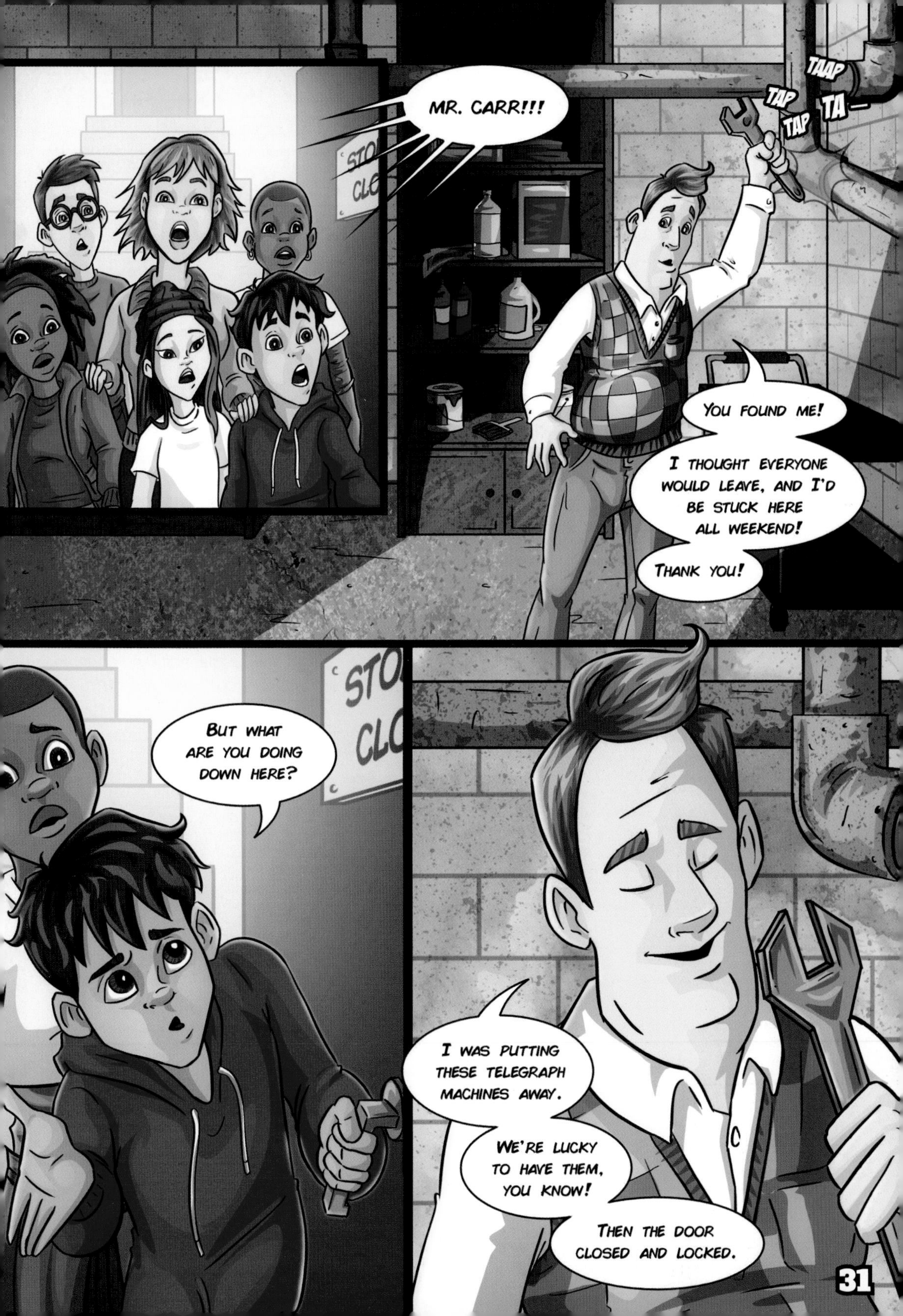
MR. CARR!!!
TAAP
TAP
TAP
TA
You found me!
I thought everyone would leave, and I'd be stuck here all weekend!
Thank you!
But what are you doing down here?
I was putting these telegraph machines away.
We're lucky to have them, you know!
Then the door closed and locked.

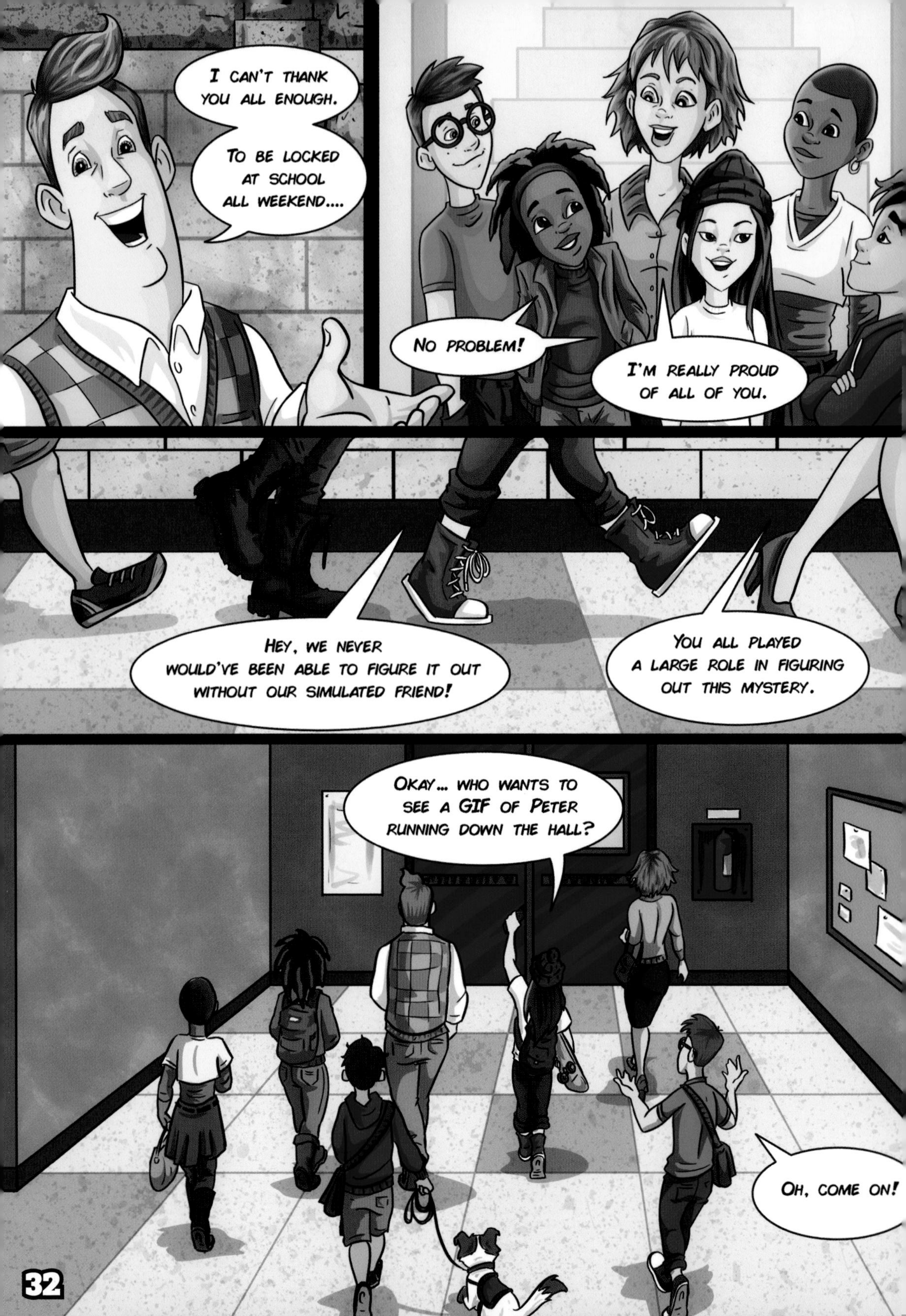
I CAN'T THANK YOU ALL ENOUGH.
TO BE LOCKED AT SCHOOL ALL WEEKEND....
NO PROBLEM!
I'M REALLY PROUD OF ALL OF YOU.
HEY, WE NEVER WOULD'VE BEEN ABLE TO FIGURE IT OUT WITHOUT OUR SIMULATED FRIEND!
YOU ALL PLAYED A LARGE ROLE IN FIGURING OUT THIS MYSTERY.
OKAY... WHO WANTS TO SEE A GIF OF PETER RUNNING DOWN THE HALL?
OH, COME ON!